Pangaea

Illustrated
Tales From an Alternate
Steampunk History
Book 3

2nd Edition

Timothy M Dooley

Pangaea: Illustrated Tales From An Alternate Steampunk History" series. It is the second installment in "The Adventures of Captain Lionheart" series and continues from where "Two Ships" left off, in the Alpha Centauri System. It is based on a short story that first posted in 2012.

All of the books in this series are dedicated to all who enjoy science fiction and especially to those who remember Jules Verne and are into Steampunk.

Sincerely-

Timothy M Dooley

"Your life is on a path, Captain, one which you must follow. It is one which will have an influence on all of humanity."

Hectra West, Proxima b, 1627

Live Islands

Captain's Log: Our voyage elapsed time is now 74 days (Sept 8, 1627, Earth Time). Because of the time storm we passed through, our actual launch date from Earth (January 1880) is now 253 years in the future. It will be that long before anyone even knows we are out here. This ship (The Onyx Tower) may very well be the most isolated ship in history. As ship's Captain, I have done my best to hide my inner feelings of uncertainty from the crew. That is, all except West. I think she can see right through me. Even though we are only a few light years from Earth, I feel completely cut off. If we made a fantastic discovery, there's no one on Earth to send a message too.

Having re-visited Proxima b, Our next port of call will be the moon of Dark Neptune. It is a part of a double planet system that circles Centauri A. Despite Proxima being a part of the Alpha Centauri star system, the other stars, Centauri A & B, are 13,000 AU's away. It was necessary to initiate a miniature space wave to arrive in Centauri A's system in just 21 hours travel time. Unlike Proxima Centauri, the other two stars of Alpha Centauri have mostly asteroids and planetoids orbiting them. I think it is because when they are at their closest distance, 11.2 AU's, their opposing gravitational pulls create a slingshot effect that causes a planet of significant mass to be thrown off into space. It is only a theory of mine.

An incredible discovery was made on my first voyage to Alpha Centauri A. We never reported it to anyone on Earth until we had a chance to return to investigate further. When we first arrived, we charted four planetoids circling the star. The unusual orbit of the planetoid in the second orbit caught our interest. We christened it "Neutron". Neutron's orbital path suggested it was circling around a much larger invisible planet of greater mass. At the time, the crew and I thought Neutron might be orbiting a micro black hole. Neutron was behaving more like a moon. It was decided we would land there to investigate further but as we approached, the faint outline of a large sphere became visible in the area Neutron was orbiting.

Also, at the same time, a double planet system, consisting of two mini-Neptune's appeared inside the sphere. No one knew what to make of it at first. The planets inside the sphere became more visible as we got closer. To confirm what we were observing was a sphere, we circled around it several times. It's diameter measured 178,935.5 miles [287,969.85 kilometers]. The Elizabeth had a brief power loss when we entered the sphere. When we did so, the double planetary system became clearly visible. So far, we have been unable to determine if the sphere field is natural or not.

We christened it the Gemini system. It is composed of two Neptune sized gas dwarf's that are locked in a tight orbit around each other. One has a ring and the other has a watery moon that is the approximate size of Earth. What makes the system interesting is the watery moon is kept in the constant shadow of the planet it orbits. If not, it most likely would have become another Venus with a hellishly hot atmosphere. We christened it's host planet Gemini B and the ringed twin Gemini A. For lack of a better term, the watery moon was christened Dark Neptune. In spite of almost being in constant darkness, Dark Neptune is warm enough to have liquid water covering 95% of its entire surface. Of all the worlds in the Alpha Centauri system, Dark Neptune appears to have the highest concentration of extraterrestrial life discovered so far. The first mission I made here 11 years ago in the Elizabeth was cut short when a sea creature attacked the ship and nearly dragged it under. Now, in a much larger ship that is able to defend itself, I hope to study this world much more closely.

Peter M. Lionheart: Captain

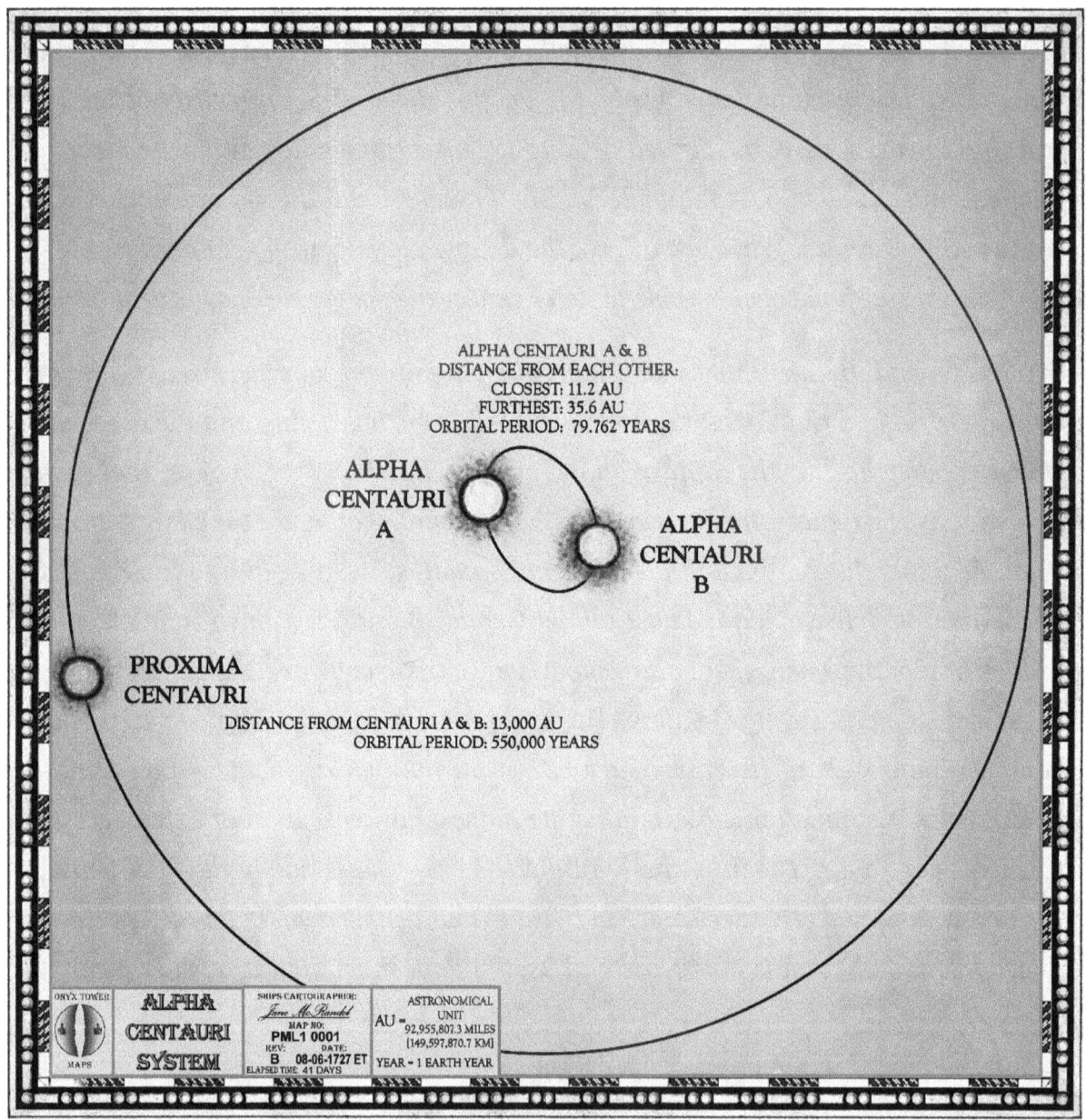

1. ALTHOUGH NOT TO SCALE, chart PML1 0001 shows the approximate orbits of the stars in the Alpha Centauri system.

2. PML1A 0001, The solar system of Alpha Centauri A. The Gemini double planet system is shown even though only the moon of Neutron is visible from interstellar space. On the chart that was revealed to Earth after Lionheart's first visit, only Neutron was shown in the second orbit.

3. JUST OUTSIDE THE ORBIT of Neutron, the Gemini double planet system starts to become visible as the Onyx Tower approaches.

4. **THE ONYX TOWER** approaches the Gemini double planet system with the moon of Dark Neptune becoming clearly visible.

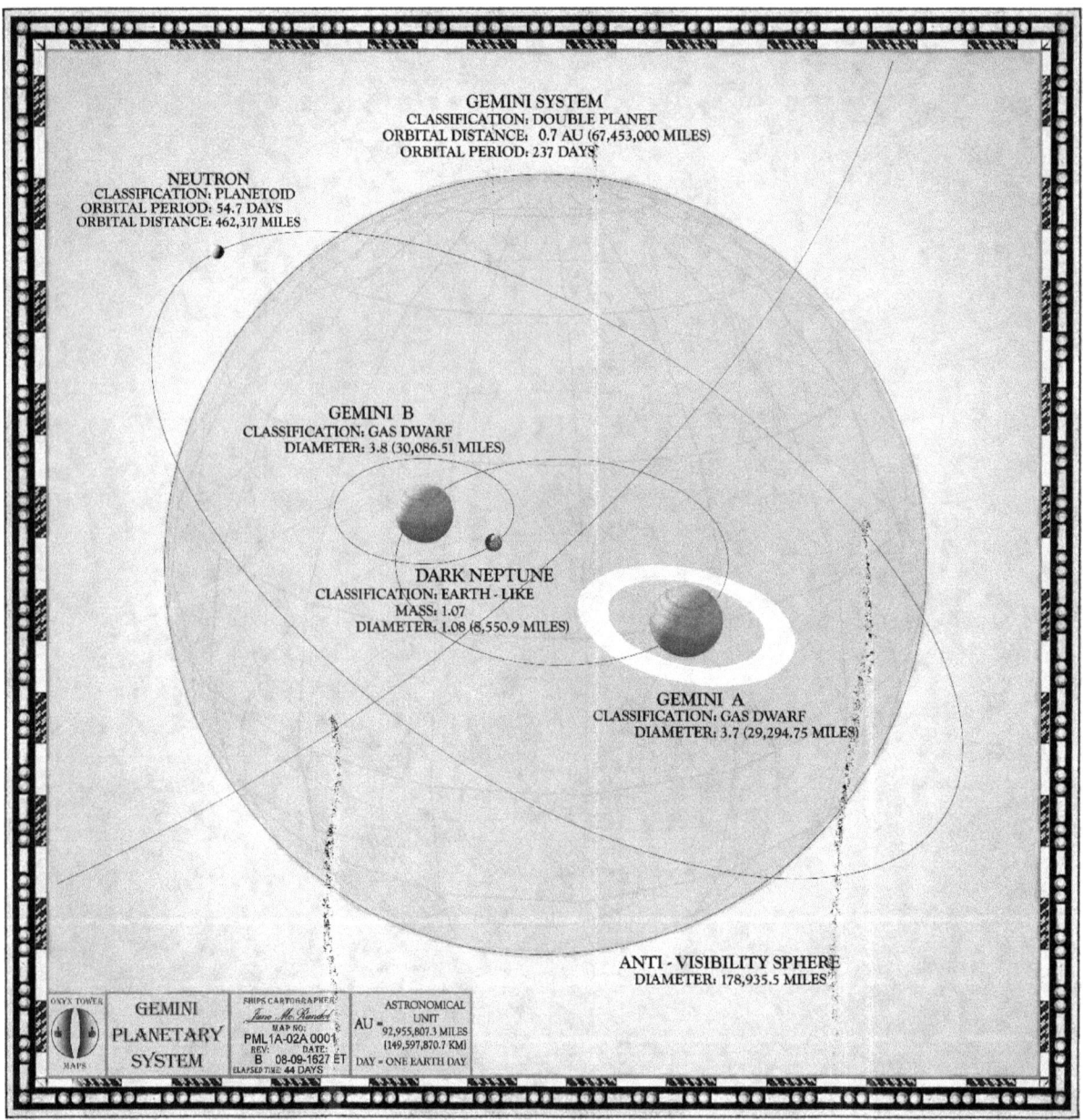

5. **THE GEMINI PLANETERY SYSTEM** chart as rendered by ship's cartographer, Jane McRandel, that was based on Lionheart's private notes from the Elizabeth's voyage.

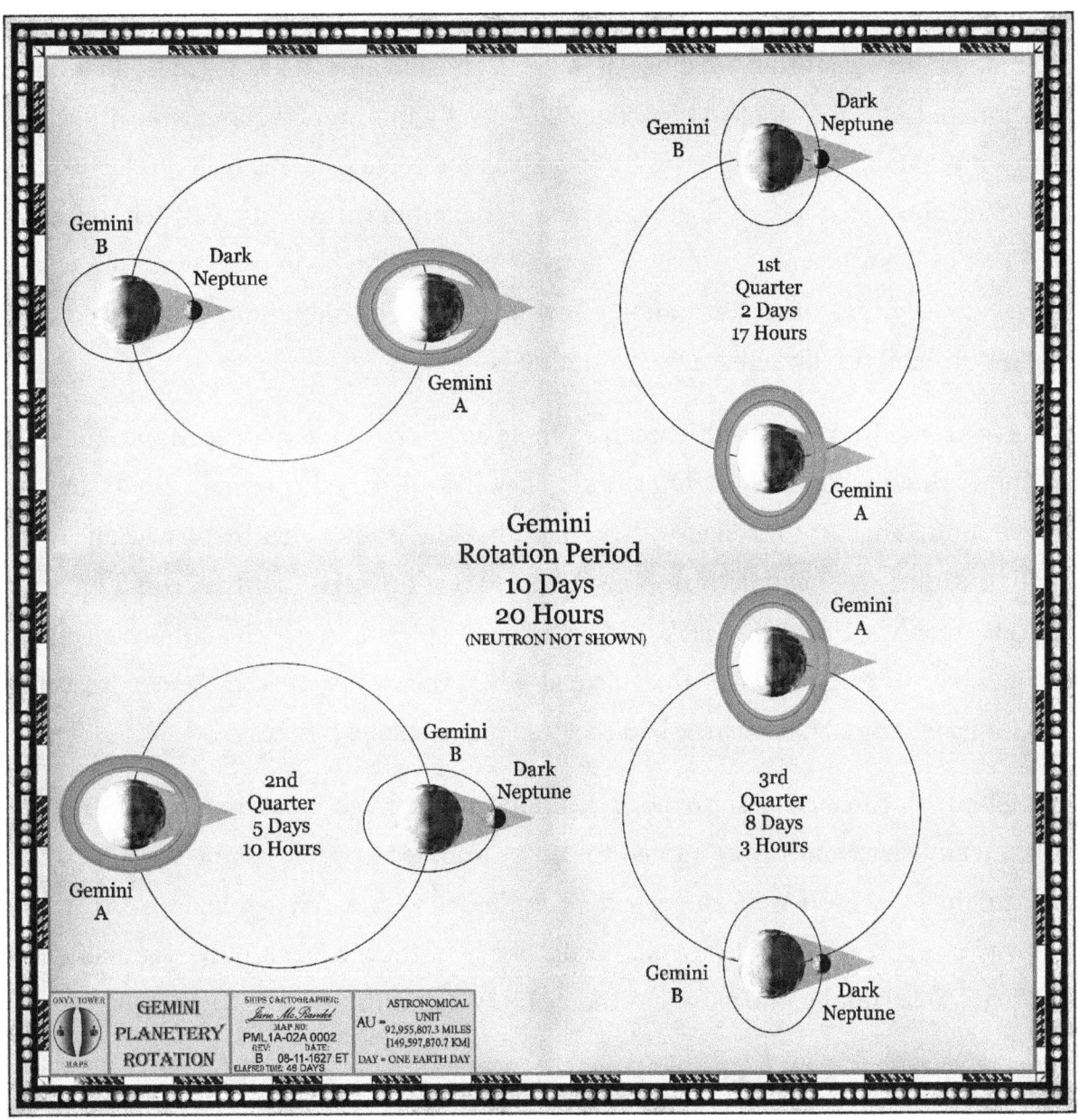

Gemini
B

Dark
Neptune

Gemini
A

Gemini
Rotation Period
10 Days
20 Hours
(NEUTRON NOT SHOWN)

Dark
Neptune

Gemini
B

1st
Quarter
2 Days
17 Hours

Gemini
A

Gemini
A

2nd
Quarter
5 Days
10 Hours

Gemini
B

Dark
Neptune

Gemini
A

3rd
Quarter
8 Days
3 Hours

Gemini
A

Gemini
B

Dark
Neptune

ONYX TOWER

GEMINI
PLANETERY
ROTATION

MAPS

SHIPS CARTOGRAPHER:
Jane Mc Randel
MAP NO:
PML1A-02A 0002
REV: DATE:
B   08-11-1627 ET
ELAPSED TIME: 46 DAYS

ASTRONOMICAL
UNIT
AU = 92,955,807.3 MILES
[149,597,870.7 KM]
DAY = ONE EARTH DAY

6. **THE SHADOWY ORBIT** of Dark Neptune was a mystery to Captain Lionheart. Given the moon's mass, its proximity to Gemini B and the rotation period, Dark Neptune should not always remain in the shadow. Some unknown force was keeping it in place. Gemini A's ring and Dark Neptune have approximately the same mass. Note: Both the ring and the orbit of Dark Neptune are elliptical.

After entering Dark Neptune's atmosphere, Lionheart had the Onyx Tower hover at a thousand feet. The placid ocean waters below extended out into the horizon all around. As the haunting memory if his first visit came back to him, Lionheart remembered how the calm waters concealed deadly monsters lurking beneath. There were some small, scattered islands off in the distance. He gave the order to have Onyx Tower set down at standard floating depth, not far from them. Lionheart felt, once the ship was in the water, it was likely a monster like the one he first encountered would appear shortly thereafter. But, after a few hours, underwater sensors detected only schools of small fish like creatures swimming below.

The sensors also revealed the ocean at their location was very deep, approximately six miles [nine point seven kilometers]. They also detected thermal activity on the ocean floor. What was unusual was the fact that the islands nearby turned out to be floating with no connection to the ocean floor. West deduced that they could have air pockets. Lionheart recalled, back on Earth, some volcanic rocks floated because they had bubbles of trapped gases that formed when they were molten. Sensor readings also indicated the islands nearby had rocky soil, and sparse tree cover.

"Captain, ships sensors show no indication of any large creatures in the area for miles in any direction. If you wanted to gather samples from the island trees, perhaps now might be a good time to send an amphibian with a science team. Also, I just received a report from Dr. Connors. According to it, the air is not only breathable but safe with no harmful pathogens detected," Mrs. West said.

"I was curious about the atmosphere the first time I came here. How is it possible for a water planet or moon to have a breathable atmosphere when there is no forest of any kind large enough to produce oxygen. We also recorded this on my first voyage, but the ship was attacked before we could study it further," Lionheart said.

"I have detected an unusually high oxygen reading in the area around those islands. Perhaps they are the source. As I stated, with the absence of any activity in the area, now might be a good time to explore them," West said.

"Yes, I know. I just want to be sure. If one of those things comes around, the amphibian wouldn't stand a chance. They would be dragged under before they knew what hit them," Lionheart said.

"Captain, we're more than willing to take the risk. This is what we came out here for," science officer Burkeman said.

"I have a feeling I'm going to hear that expression many times before this ship has reached the end of its voyage." Lionheart said quietly to himself.

"Sir, if sensors detected anything large enough to be what attacked the Elizabeth, it would still take several minutes to reach our position. That would allow more than enough time to move the Tower into position where it could protect and retrieve the landing party. Since are arrival, several unusual trace elements have been detected in the islands proximity. Their presence has aroused my scientific curiosity. I would also like to join the away team." West said.

"Very well West, but at the first sign of..."

"I know Captain. Since I'm directly tied into the ships systems, I will be the first to know", West said interrupting Lionheart.

A short time later, Burkeman, biologist Colman, botanist Sibiu, and West entered the amphibian and sealed the hatches. Looking down into the launch bay, chief engineer Petrov gave the order to flood the bay and open the outer doors. As the amphibian was released from its mooring, Lionheart came up behind Petrov. Not saying anything, he quietly clenched his fists as he watched the amphibian leave the bay into the dark water beyond. Petrov could see Lionheart was very unsettled. He heard Lionheart's story of what the Elisabeth had encountered and wondered if they would encounter the same monster.

"Mr. Petrov, leave the bay doors open. If the away team has to make it back in a hurry, I don't want anything to slow them down," Lionheart said.

"Are you expecting trouble Captain?" Petrov asked.

"Let's hope not...", Lionheart said as he left the launch bay.

7. **DEPARTING THE ONYX TOWER'S** launch bay, the lone amphibian made its way out into the waters of Dark Neptune to investigate the floating islands nearby.

"Mr. Quinn, do you have anything out there?" Lionheart asked as he entered the bridge.

"Only the islands and the away team, Captain. Beyond that, sensors show we are clear, sir," Quinn responded.

"Very good. I won't rest until their back," Lionheart said quietly.

"Yes Sir. I'll keep monitoring."

"All right Quinn. Mr. Thornton, I want a rotorcraft equipped with a lightning cannon readied and sent up right away," Lionheart said as he sat down watching the ships viewing screens.

"Aye sir, Peterson is our best pilot. I'll have him fly the mission", Thornton responded.

In the dark waters outside the ship, the amphibian surfaced. Moving slowly, it made its way to the shore of the nearest island and came up on the land. With the exception of a few stark trees, the island seemed barren. One by one, West and the others climbed out of the amphibian. Considering the fact that Dark Neptune was always in a shadow, the air seemed unusually warm and humid. Not wasting any time, the team began collecting samples. Everyone was bathed in the blue light of the ringed gas giant, Gemini A, in the horizon. It was much brighter than a full moon on Earth.

In his rotorcraft, Peterson lifted off from the Onyx Tower and headed toward the island. Once there, he circled around it, always keeping the away team in full view. While the others tried to collect soil samples from the hard ground, West and Burkeman examined the trees. As they got closer, West detected a significant rise in oxygen levels, far beyond that of any normal Earthly vegetation. Just as Burkeman was about to cut off a sample of leaves, West motioned him to stop.

"What is it, West?" He asked.

"Just a moment", West said as she stepped closer. Leaning in, she examined the tree further. As she held up a small group of leaves, West adjusted her eyes to high magnification. Even though the light from Gemini A was bright, West's eyes lit up to study the leaves even closer. What she saw confirmed her suspicions. The leaf tissue was more like the capillary tissue found in animal lungs. The tree they were examining wasn't a tree at all, but rather a kind of lung turned inside out. Without warning, Burkeman cut off a small sample. Immediately, there was an earthquake! It was so sudden and violent that everyone fell to the ground.

"That was foolish! You shouldn't have done that!", West said, as she scolded Burkeman.

"I thought you were finished", he said as he got to his feet.

"It is no longer safe here! We must return to the ship at once," West commanded.

"Mrs. West, our sensors detected tremors on your island! What is going on out there?" Lionheart asked.

"Captain, I think we have awakened the island! We are returning to the ship as soon as possible," West said, as they everyone started running back to the amphibian.

"Captain, sensors indicate the surrounding islands are also beginning to have tremors. Their frequency matched that of the away team's island," Quinn said.

"Tower, Peterson here, the sea around the islands is really getting churned up! It's starting to get rough down there!"

From Peterson's nose camera, Lionheart and the others could see everyone running back to the amphibian. In a frantic hurry, the landing party boarded the amphibian and backed off the island. As they entered the water, the island listed to one side like a large animal trying to shake something off its back. The amphibian was violently plunged into the water. West and the others were knocked around inside. It took a moment to regain themselves. Once they did, the amphibian made its way back to the

Onyx Tower at full speed. They quickly submerged to avoid the violent, churned up surface water.

8. **AS THE AMPHIBIAN ENTERED THE WATER,** the island rolled to one side like a large animal trying to shake something off its back.

"Captain, sensors are picking up movement of a large body coming from below. Its depth is approximately a thousand meters. Tremors from the islands may have stirred something up. Sir, whatever it is, it is headed to the surface and it's coming fast!" Quinn reported.

"Burkeman, this is Lionheart. We have detected something closing in on our position. Get back here as fast as you can!" Lionheart commanded.

"Sir, the body is now at 700 meters! They're not going to make it back in time!" Quinn reported.

"Burkeman, this is Lionheart, I want you to run on the surface until reaching the tower!"

"Sir, we'll make better time submerged!" Burkeman reported.

"He's right sir," Quinn responded.

"Burkeman, I can't protect you unless you surface," Lionheart said.

"He's right, ship's sensors have detected something very large approaching," West said, sitting directly behind Burkeman.

"Peterson, I want your cannon trained on the area around the amphibian as soon it surfaces!" Lionheart commanded.

"Captain, sensors indicate the body is now at three hundred meters and coming up on the far side of the island. Sir, if Peterson fires his cannon near the amphibian, the discharge could short out its systems," Quinn said.

"I'm aware of that. That is a risk I'll have to take."

"Sir, the amphibian is surfacing!" Peterson reported.

"Very good. Stay on them Peterson," Lionheart commanded.

"Captain, sensors are now picking up a second large body coming up from below. It is now at twelve hundred meters and rising! Quinn reported.

"Great, that's all we need, a feeding frenzy," first officer, Thornton said.

"Sir the first large body is now very close to the surface! It is passing under the island now. My guess is, once it passes under the island, it will surface just before attacking the landing party!" Quinn said.

"Peterson, I want you to hover over the amphibian and train your cannon on the area behind it. A creature is closing fast, and I think that's where it will surface!" Lionheart commanded.

"Aye sir. I'm ready," Peterson responded.

A large sea creature surfaced not from the island, heading directly for the amphibian. As he watched the event on Peterson's camera, a cold chill came over Lionheart. He briefly re-lived a memory when a similar creature attacked the Elizabeth and almost dragged it under. Peterson aimed his cannon at the approaching creature, but seconds before he could fire, the island suddenly turned and lunged toward the creature. To everyone's shock and horror, the island revealed what looked like four, yellow glowing eyes and a grand mouth, lined with pointed, stone like teeth. It an instant, it was upon the creature and swallowed it whole. The island's sudden movement caused a large wave of water to crash over the amphibian and eventually strike the Onyx Tower. Having consumed the sea creature, the island became still again.

9. **TO EVERYONE'S SHOCK AND HORROR,** the island was in fact a living creature.

"Christ All Mighty!" Lionheart said to himself.

"Well, it would seem the sea creature you encountered earlier was not at the top of the food chain here," Thornton said.

"Evidently not," Lionheart responded.

"Captain, the amphibian is submerging to enter the launch bay. They're almost back sir," Quinn said.

"Good, the sooner the better. Mr. Petrov, let me know the moment you have them, and the launch bay is secure," Lionheart commanded.

"Aye Captain, they are coming in now sir," Petrov responded.

"Captain, the second large body we detected is now at 250 meters and is moving in an upward spiral between the Tower and the island creature," Quinn reported.

"Mr. Peterson, increase your altitude to a thousand feet and adjust your camera to wide angle. We have detected a second, larger sea creature below. I want to see if we can get some images of it as it surfaces," Lionheart said.

"Aye, sir. Increasing altitude now," Peterson responded.

"Oh my God!" Quinn said, as sensors detected the second creature lunging toward the surface. Before he could react, the snake like creature blasted up out of the water, grabbed the rotorcraft in its mouth and lunged back down into the sea.

"Captain! It all happened so quickly Sir! The second creature was well below the surface when it suddenly lunged upward! Before I could say anything, it had Peterson!" Quinn said.

"It's alright Quinn, I was also taken by surprise the first time I came here. What is the creature doing now?" Lionheart asked.

"It's not diving. It's swimming just below the surface away from here. Wait, sensors indicate it is now moving off to the northeast. I'm still receiving the locater signal from Peterson's rotorcraft," Quinn said.

"That's a good thing. It means the rotorcraft hasn't been crushed by that creature's jaws. Has the creature changed depth?" Thornton asked.

"No sir, it's just below the surface, maintaining an approximate depth of 9 meters. It's starting to increase speed."

10. BEFORE PETERSON COULD REACT, the snake like creature blasted up out of the water, grabbed the rotorcraft in its mouth and lunged back down into the sea.

"Mr. Quinn, bring the tower up to 500 feet. Lock on to Peterson's signal and pursue," Lionheart commanded.

"Captain, if the creature returns to the depths, retrieving Peterson alive might be impossible. The rotorcraft was not designed to handle that kind of pressure," Thornton said.

"I know. If we try to use any of our weapons, Peterson could be killed. I have to think of something fast," Lionheart said.

"Captain, the creature is maintaining a speed of 43 knots. We are closing. We are almost on top of him. The creature is now starting to dive. I think it may be aware of our presence sir," Quinn reported.

"Mr. Quinn, back us off to a distance of five miles," Lionheart commanded.

"Aye Sir, backing off to five miles. Sir, Sensors indicate the area is beginning to shallow and there is a submerged island approximately seven miles ahead. The creature appears to be coming back up. It's now running just under the surface, sir," Quinn reported.

"You were right about the creature being spooked. How did you know?" Thornton asked.

"I didn't. It was just a guess. I have the feeling the creature didn't grab the rotorcraft for itself," Lionheart said.

"Why would you say that?"

"Because if he wanted it for himself, he could have crushed the rotorcraft in his powerful jaws and swallowed it whole. I have a hunch," Lionheart quietly said to Thornton.

"Sir, the area is still shallowing. Sensors indicate the submerged island ahead is only about 15 meters below the surface. Captain, the island appears to have several organic formations growing around it's perimeter. The creature has reached the island and entered the formation area. It appears to be heading towards the island's interior," Quinn said.

11. WITH THE AMPHIBIAN RECOVERED, the Onyx Tower lifted up out of the water in pursuit of the monster carrying the rotorcraft with Peterson.

The submerged island ahead of them was dominated by a circular row of tall, steep rock like pillars that stood like powerful majestic sentinels, protecting the island's center from open water. Each of them stood hundreds of feet into the air. They reminded Lionheart of Stonehenge, back in England. Positioned several hundred feet apart, the space between them was enough for a large ship to pass thru.

"Thornton, what do you make of that?" Lionheart asked, as they looked out over the formations.

"I don't know. They look more like the rotted wood remains from some gigantic forest. Their general shape and size reminds me of an area off the south coast of China," Thornton said.

"Sir, the creature has reached the center of the formation area. Just a moment. It's stopped, no, it's moving off. It is now heading out of the formation area out the far side and leaving the island. Captain! Peterson's signal is still coming from somewhere near the center of the open area. The creature must have dropped him there, sir!" Quinn said, in a raised voice.

"What now Captain?" Thornton asked.

"Now, we get our man back. Mr. Quinn, get us as close to the signal as you can," Lionheart commanded.

"We are approaching the center of the island now, sir, Quinn said.

There was a small mound at the area's center. Lionheart and the others couldn't tell what it was composed of until they got closer and could see it was the chopped up remains of dead creatures, like the one that attacked the Elizabeth. They could see Peterson's rotorcraft resting on the rim of the dead pile.

"Captain, I have a bad feeling about this," Thornton said.

"I know. I think all those carcasses were put there for a reason. Like worms brought to a bird's nest back on Earth, those bodies were placed there to feed the creatures unborn. We may not have much time," Lionheart said.

"Aye Captain," Thornton responded.

"Mr. Quinn. Take us out to where the water is deep enough and lower the tower to minimum launch bay depth. Mr. Thornton. Put together a four-man landing party. We are going to grapple the rotorcraft to an amphibian and tow it back to the launch bay," Lionheart commanded.

"Captain, I would like to lead the landing party," West requested as she entered the bridge.

"Request denied. West, I believe the metal alloy body of the rotorcraft was what attracted the creature in the first place. I'm afraid if you go out there, the same thing could happen to you. I can't risk it. Mr. Thornton, I want you to lead the landing party and take Ross with you," Lionheart said.

"Aye Captain," Thornton responded.

"Well, at least have a hanson go with the team. I can quickly have a coating applied to its armor that will temporarily mask its metallic properties," West responded.

"Very well, the hanson will accompany the team," Lionheart said.

Not far from the area's center, the Onyx Tower slowly dropped into the water. It had the appearance of a floating castle with gentle waves lapping against its walls.

"We are at minimum launch bay depth, Captain. This is as close as we can get without running aground. The rotorcraft signal is just over a mile away," Quinn said.

"Alright. Very good Quinn," Lionheart said as Thornton left the bridge.

A short time later, Lionheart and the others watched as the amphibian departed from the partly submerged launch bay.

"Captain, sensors are detecting small movements coming from all directions. It may be nothing. I suspect they were caused when we first sat the ship down in the water, sir," Quinn reported.

As Thornton's party got closer to Peterson's rotorcraft, the ground became shallow enough for the amphibian to bottom out on its treads. Continuing further, the vehicle began to rise higher out of the water. It was like moving over a thick mud. Thornton could see part of the rotorcraft resting above the water. Looking around, Thornton and Ross were somewhat startled by piles of dead creatures. They all got out when they reached the rotorcraft. The water was just above waist height. Thornton was glad they were wearing environment suits. He imagined the stench from the dead creatures must be overwhelming. Looking through the rotorcraft window, Thornton could see that Peterson was still alive, but barely moving. The hatch was jammed shut when the creature bit down on the vehicle. Thornton knew Peterson didn't have much time until his air supply ran out.

"Mr. Thornton, the best place to attach the cables is on the underside of the rotorcraft, sir" Ross said.

"No problem, I can reach it," the hanson said, as it knelt down below the waterline.

Thornton and Ross stepped back as they watched the hanson slowly roll the craft over and get back to his feet. Thornton was never sure, but he earlier estimated a hanson robot had the approximate strength of thirty men.

"Captain, signals from small movements all around are steadily increasing, sir. The water movement isn't coming from us. There is something else out here," Quinn reported.

12. **IN A RACE AGAINST TIME** the amphibian moved as fast as they could to reach Peterson before his air supply ran out. **ABOVE:** As the amphibian came closer Thornton, and the others could see the rotorcraft had been placed among the remains of many dead creatures. **BELOW:** Inside the rotorcraft, crewmen Peterson was unconscious but still alive.

"Mr. Thornton. How's your progress out there. Sensors indicate the creature's young may be hatching," Lionheart said.

"We are just about finished now sir. The hanson is attaching the last cable, and Ross is collecting a tissue sample from the dead creatures," Thornton reported.

"Tissue samples?" Lionheart asked.

"Yes sir. Just as we were boarding the amphibian, Dr. Connors approached Ross and asked him to get a small tissue sample from a creature if possible. He's got it and is coming back now. The hanson has just finished," Thornton said.

As they started to board the amphibian, two newborn creatures attacked the hanson's legs.

"Thornton! Ross! Get aboard now and close yourself in! I'll take care of these," the hanson said, as it tore the creatures away from its legs and flung them away. It climbed up on the amphibian and pounded on its outer hull, signaling Thornton to get moving.

Not wasting any time, Thornton backed away as fast as he could. Soon after, the amphibian was once again floating in deep water. Thornton quickly turned it around and started to make his way back to the tower with the rotorcraft in tow. At the same time, the hanson kept fighting off the newly hatched creatures. Every time it pulled one off and threw it away, more would come up out of the water, trying to bite. Thornton and Ross believed the creatures were attracted to the hanson's metal skin. The amphibian and rotorcraft were also attacked, but not enough the stop them from returning to the tower. Just before reaching the launch bay the amphibian submerged. With all the newborn creatures swimming around them, the amphibian and rotorcraft had the general appearance of a school of fish as they entered the launch bay.

13. **WITH ALL THE NEWBORN CREATURES** swimming around them, the amphibian and rotorcraft had the general appearance of a school of fish as they entered the launch bay.

"Captain, we have the away team and Peterson, but the launch bay is swarming with those newborn creatures. I don't know how we are going to clear them out of the launch bay," Petrov reported.

Deep in thought, Lionheart was silent for a moment. "Mr. Thornton. Have the hanson grab and lock his hands in place on to the amphibian. Then have him shut down," Lionheart commanded.

"Aye sir," Thornton responded.

Moments later Petrov could see the red light in the hanson's eyes go out.

"Captain, the amphibian is secure, and the hanson is shut down," Thornton reported.

"Very good. I'm going to release a static discharge in the launch bay, "Lionheart said.

"Captain. The landing party can insulate themselves, but Peterson may be at risk. If I may suggest, slowly raise the Tower to altitude. I don't think those creatures can be out of the water for long," West said.

"You may be right. Mr. Quinn. Take us up on a slow assent to a thousand feet," Lionheart said after pausing for a moment.

Aye Sir," Quin responded.

Frightened by the first deep pulse from the Onyx Tower's engine, several creatures stopped their attack and swam out of the launch bay. Flowing like a river, water began to rush out of the bay doors. As it poured down into the sea below, more creatures broke away. The Onyx Tower was now completely out of the water.

"Five hundred feet," Quinn reported.

The air in the launch bay was starting to become cold and windy. One by one, more creatures crawled to the bay door and jumped out. Inside the amphibian, it became quiet. The tapping sounds of the creatures biting against the hull had stopped.

"One thousand feet and holding, sir," Quinn reported.

"Very good Mr. Quinn," Lionheart responded.

"Captain. I think that may be the last of them. We don't see any of them in our windows," Thornton said.

"I don't see anything either, sir," Petrov reported.

"Mr. Quinn. Take us up to 100,000 feet. Mr. Petrov. Close bay doors and pressurize. Have your team put on environment suits before entering the bay and take two security men armed with electric guns," Lionheart commanded.

"Captain. What is your plan?" West asked.

"In the event, they run into another one of those creatures, we can quickly depressurize the bay if we need to," Lionheart said.

"I have my concerns, Captain. Normally the rotorcraft can hold cabin pressure without any problem, however Peterson's hatch may have been compromised when the creature bit down on it. I would suggest turning the hanson back on and having two more of his kind inspect the bay," West said.

"Point taken West. Mr. Quinn. Stop our assent and hold at present altitude. Mr. Thornton. Wake the hanson up and instruct it to inspect the launch bay," Lionheart commanded.

"Captain?" came Dr. Connors voice over the com.

"Yes doctor, what is it?" Lionheart responded.

"If there are any creatures still in the launch bay, I would like one captured, preferably alive, if possible," Connors requested.

"I was so worried about Peterson, I forgot we came out here to study all alien life," Lionheart said quietly to himself. "Very well doctor. If there are any left, well try to capture one alive if possible."

The hanson was turned back on and joined by two others, Hanson3 and Hanson7. Moving very carefully, the three searched the launch bay. At first it appeared there were no creatures, until Henson3's left arm was bitten off when he squatted down in front of the amphibian. A wounded creature was hiding between the vehicle's treads. As a result, from its wounds, it was far more aggressive than the others. Its tail had snagged on the amphibian's treads with it first entered the bay. At first there was little the hanson's could do to subdue the creature. The amphibian's treads gave it just enough protection where it could easily defend itself. Also, it's almost metal like skin was far too tough for any hypodermic spear to penetrate. At one point during the standoff, the first hanson and Hanson3 tried to distract the creature while Hanson7 tried to seize it from the rear. The attempt only resulted in Hanson7 losing its right hand. After that, the hansons backed away and stood motionless.

"What is happening? Why are they backing away?" Lionheart asked himself quietly.

"Captain. I have instructed the hansons to back away and await further orders. My analysis of Dark Neptune's climate patterns is now complete. It seems there is a period that occurs once every seven of its years where the entire moon essentially becomes a great ball of ice," West reported.

"What does that have to do with what is going on here?" Lionheart asked.

"I believe all animal life on this moon has the ability to go into a deep state of hibernation. This would allow it to survive this period. If the launch bay temperature were lowered to -250°F [-157°C], it would simulate the same conditions of this cold period. I think, once exposed to this condition, the creature should go into a state of hibernation. Once it is in that state, the hansons would have little trouble retrieving the creature. Also, because our vehicles are so well insulated, the drop in temperature should have little or no effect on Peterson or Thornton's team." West said.

"Well, it's worth a try. Mr. Petrov. Lower the launch bay temperature to -250°F," Lionheart ordered.

"Aye, but Captain, I'm curious as to why?" Petrov asked.

"I'll explain later Petrov," Lionheart responded.

"Aye Captain."

West was right. Less than an hour after the temperature dropped, the creature went into a state of hibernation. It was later taken from the launch bay and placed in a small swimming pool, enclosed by thick glass walls referred to as "The Tank". Lionheart had it built to observe alien marine life. It was inspired by the earlier discoveries on Europa. Later, after the temperature in the launch bay rose above freezing, Thornton's team emerged from the amphibian and Peterson was finally rescued from the rotorcraft. He was shaken up but would recover in a few days. Five days later, after Connors felt her analyses was complete, the creature was released back into the sea. She did, however, collect several small tissue samples for further study. To everyone's surprise, Mr. Ivanov (the Russian survivor that was picked up from the last departure point back on Earth), showed a keen interest in the study of alien life. Dr. Connors felt he had a remarkable aptitude for biology, in spite of the fact that he had been a mechanical engineer.

14. ALEXI IVANOV, the Russian that had been rescued from Western Siberia, had technical skills far greater than anyone knew. Without anyone's knowledge, he altered one of the hanson units to secretly retrieve one of the infant creatures. After receiving it, he was able to keep it in a suspended sleep and stored in a hidden place aboard the tower.

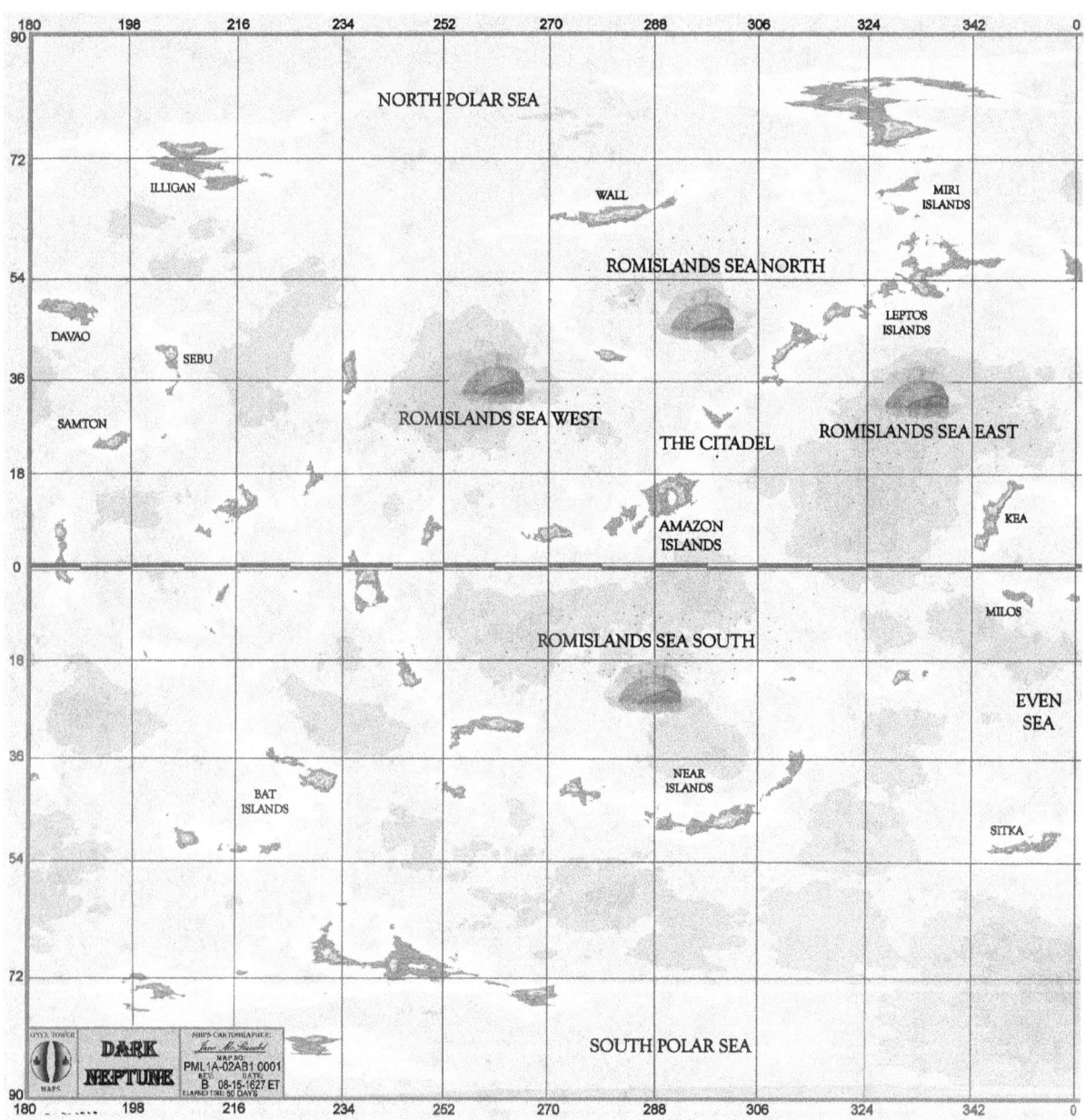

15. **AFTER THE RESCUE OF CREWMEN PETERSON,** the Onyx Tower charted the moon of Dark Neptune. Lionheart ordered ship's cartographer Jane McRandel to make a formal map. Because the exploration was somewhat brief, only a few islands were named. The seas named with "Romislands" meant areas inhabited with the large island creatures.

34

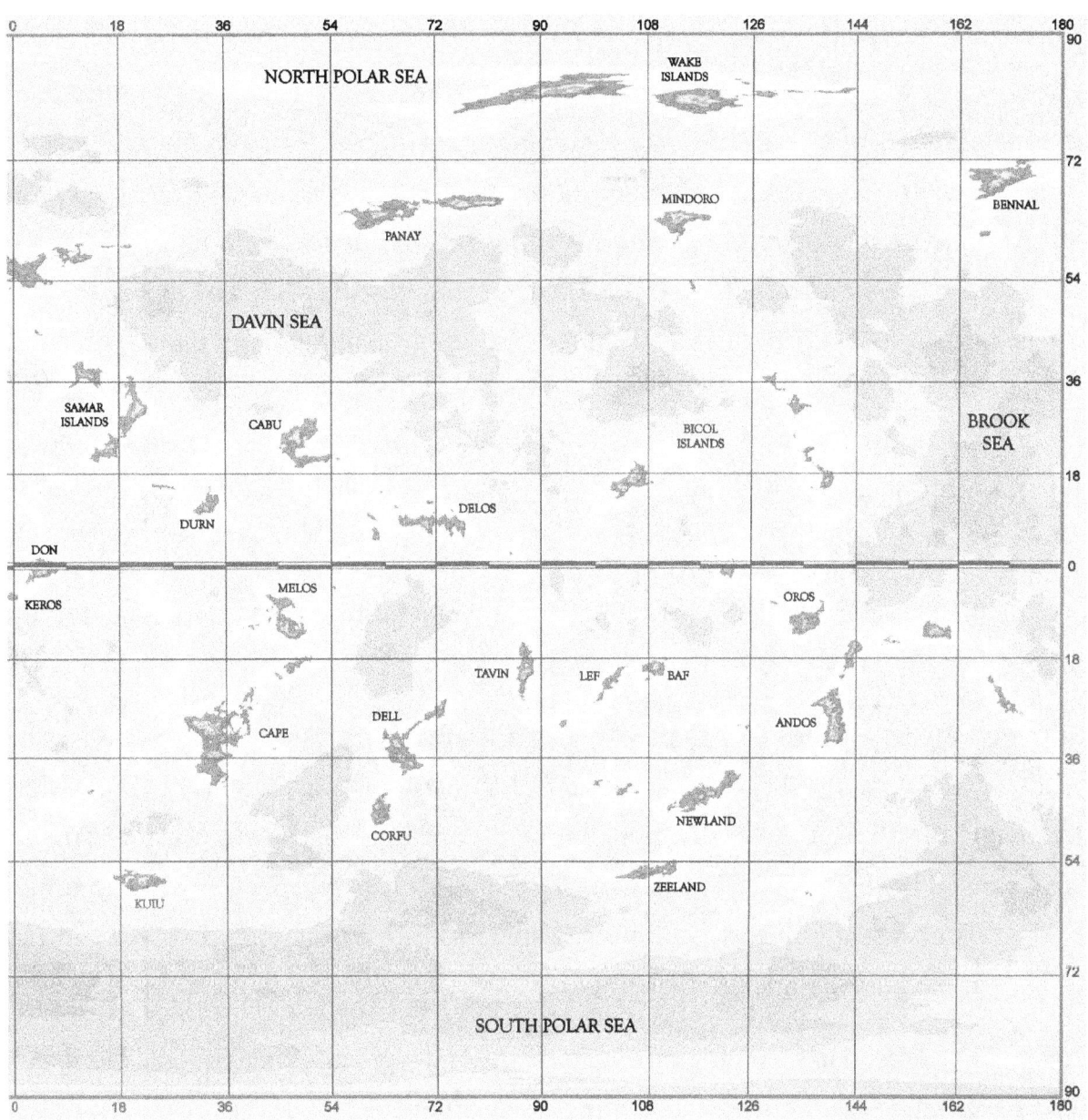

Departure

Captain's Log: Our voyage elapsed time is now 88 days (Sept 22, 1627, Earth Time). After the "Peterson Incident", as it was later referred to, we managed to closely observe and study the more dominant creatures in Dark Neptune's food chain. Having completed the mapping of the moon's oceans, I'm now satisfied with all we have learned from the Alpha Centauri system, at least for now. The space wave has been initiated and the Onyx Tower is now in route to its next destination: Barnard's Star. I expect to arrive there in approximately 23 hours. There is something to be said about the effects of moving space itself. I'm still amazed at the reality of traveling several light years in a matter of hours. I..." Lionheart stopped. He started to feel slightly dizzy. It suddenly occurred to him; his dizziness wasn't a physical condition. Something was wrong with the ship.

"Captain. Please come to the bridge at once. Something unusual is happening up here," Thornton said.

"I'm on my way Thornton," Lionheart responded as he got up from his desk. As he made his way to the bridge, he could feel himself getting lighter, then heavier. Normally, the tower's direct drive engine maintained at least a one-gravity while in space, but now there was a fluctuation. It made walking difficult. On his way to the bridge, Lionheart stumbled twice but was able to keep from falling. Everyone in the tower was having the same problem.

"Mr. Thornton. What is going on? Why is the ship's gravity fluctuating?" Lionheart asked as he and the others started floating off the floor.

"We seem to be caught in some sort of space wave fluctuation Captain. Look," Thornton said as he motioned toward the bridge view screens.

Unable to fully comprehend what he was seeing, Lionheart stood motionless for a moment as he looked out. There were patches of bright stellar gas and stars swirling around as though the ship was caught in some sort of galactic whirlpool. Normally, while riding the space wave, the stars in the forward direction would appear to be clustered in what looked like a compressed sphere. While in the opposite direction, the stars would appear to be exploding outward forming a circular ring. Lionheart began to have the impression the stars and gas were spinning around like flotsam on the water after a large ship had passed by.

"Captain, when the ship came under the effect of space distortion, we lost our navigational direction and the ship's internal drive shut down automatically. Even at a recalculation rate of 978 times per second, the ship is unable to determine our approximate position. The unknown distortion around us is too great. With the internal drive shut down and our rate of acceleration decreasing, we will be at zero gravity in approximately one minute," West said.

"This is the Captain. All crew, secure for zero gravity. Alarm will sound in one minute," Lionheart said, speaking into the com. A minute later the alarm sounded, and the hum of the internal drive engine faded. The ship was at zero gravity. It wasn't uncommon for the Onyx Tower to be at zero gravity once in space. Normally, as a precaution, there were no open containers of liquid, and most small items were kept secure, but as always, throughout the ship, there were unsecure objects and crew floating around. At that moment everyone not strapped in started floating.

"Captain?" West asked.

"Yes. I can feel it. The tower. It's starting to spin slightly in relation to the motion of the stars," Lionheart said.

"Curious," West said as she stopped to collect her thoughts. "I believe we have encountered another space wave Captain," West said. She stopped herself again to study the view outside. "Judging by the distortion and the effect it is having on the tower, I would say the space wave we encountered is far more powerful than our own."

"So, there is another ship out here," Lionheart said quietly as he continued to look out at the main view.

"So, it would seem, and judging by the disturbance, it is clearly a ship of considerable power," West said as she continued to study her console and receive direct input from the tower's sensors.

"Captain! Look!" Thornton said pointing at the forward viewing screen.

Among the oozing displays of gas and stars was a large black sphere. The absence of any surface detail gave it the appearance of a black hole. For a brief moment no one spoke, as they tried to ascertain exactly what they were observing.

"Captain, I believe that is the source of the space disturbance we are encountering," West said.

"That is the other ship?" Thornton asked.

"Yes. As far as our ships sensors can indicate, it is clearly a ship of advanced design. It measures approximately five miles in diameter. It seems we have had our first encounter with intelligent alien life or something that was created by it," West added.

As they watched, the black, alien ship grew smaller and smaller as it moved further away, continuing on its course.

"We have to investigate. West, is there any way we can catch up to it?" Lionheart asked.

"No Captain. Even with all our singularity devices on board, we could only generate a small fraction of the power necessary to reach it. The only reason we were able to observe it for this long was because we were temporarily caught up in its space wave," West explained.

16. **THERE WAS BRIEF PANDEMONIUM** on the bridge of the Onyx Tower as the ship's encounter with a powerful space wave caused a period of zero gravity.

17. LIKE FLOTSON WORRLING AROUND in the wake of a strong current, the Onyx Tower was overcome by the powerful space wave left by the alien ship.

"It's almost out of sight," Thornton said.

"Yes, and very soon the effects of its space will wear off. Captain, the result of which could be a violent shock wave. I suggest we secure the ship as much as possible," West said.

Lionheart looked at her and nodded. "Crew, this is the Captain. We have encountered a space wave from another ship. As soon as it passes, there may be a violent shock wave when we return to normal space. All sections secure the ship, and everyone is to get into space suits as soon as possible. Captain out."

Nearly an hour had passed since Lionheart gave the order to secure the ship. Earlier, the ship had been slowly turning in its central axis, but now it was also starting to spin end over end. Everyone on the bridge slowly floated up and became pressed against the ceiling. Soon after, Lionheart could tell he was at one gravity. He tried to get to his feet, but the force keeping him against the ceiling was getting stronger. The Tower was starting to spin faster and faster. "If this keeps up..." Lionheart wondered, "...at what point will the Tower tear itself in half." Seconds later, the force holding him down became so strong, he couldn't lift his head. He guessed his weight to be approximately five or six times normal. The spin continued to increase. Lionheart passed out. By now, all over the ship, the entire living crew had passed out.

Lionheart felt a strange sense of peace. He thought he could hear a voice calling him from a distance. All around, the landscape was dark. Off in the distance there was a sphere-shaped building. As far as he could tell, it was only the burned out remains of a large structure. There was a faint green light coming from inside it. It was the only source of light. It was also the source of the voice calling him. Even though he couldn't make out what it was saying, Lionheart felt it was a cry for help. As he made his way across the dark landscape the voice got louder and louder. Then it began to change. It was someone known to him. It was West. Lionheart slowly opened his eyes. He was lying on the floor of the bridge, and the visor of his helmet was open. West was down on one knee leaning over him.

"West. How long was I out?" he asked as he tried to set up. Looking around he could see the others were also starting to wake up. Lionheart could hear the sound of the internal drive engine. The ship was back at one gravity.

"You and most everyone else were unconscious for approximately 24 hours Captain. After you passed out, I ordered the mechanical crew to attend all living crew members. Once the space disturbance had passed, I slowly re-engaged the internal drive engine and set it for one gravity. That made it much easier for us to attend to the crew and inspect the ship for any damage. Fortunately, it was only minor, and the mechanical crews are making repairs as we speak. As soon as you are ready, I would like to brief the officers in the wardroom," West said as Lionheart slowly got to his feet. Looking out, he could see a green nebula directly ahead.

A short time later, all crew was fully revived. The distortion of space had ended, but it was clear they were many light years from their previous position. This was highlighted by the sight of a large green stellar nebula nearby. West addressed the officers assembled in the wardroom. "As many of you already know, we encountered a powerful space wave on our departure from the Alpha Centauri system, and as you might expect we were carried several light years off our course."

"How far Mrs. West?" Lionheart asked.

"997.78247 light years," she answered.

"We couldn't make it back to our original course even if we wanted to," Thornton said.

"I take it that you have confirmed our position? The reason I ask is that I have no knowledge of any green nebula a thousand light years from Earth. The only one I can think of offhand is somewhere over three thousand light years away," Lionheart said.

"Yes Captain, my calculations are correct. You must consider our location. I haven't determined its exact age, but so far, this nebula is relatively small and very young, only about 351.83 years. It will not be visible to the Earth for another 645.95247 years. It was part of a trinary star system not far from here," West said.

"West, you remained fully operational through this whole disturbance and had time not only to determine our position, but also study our new surroundings as well. I understand re-starting the internal drive engine made it easier to attend to the crew, but it also means we are moving thru space at a steady rate of constant acceleration. Did you set the ship's course in any specific direction?" Lionheart asked.

"Yes Captain. Ship's sensors have detected a Jovian class rogue planet 443 million miles from our initial position after the space wave passed. We are now on a direct course for it. I have determined it was once in orbit around the star that exploded into the green nebula. We should arrive at the planet in three days' time," West explained.

"Well done West," Lionheart said as he nodded with approval.

"Captain, the rogue planet's existence is not why I set course for there. After the passing of the space wave we encountered, I was able to determine its direction and its point of origin. According to my calculations, the ship we encountered came from the rogue planet we are headed for," West said.

"Well, when we first departed from Earth, I had a strong feeling we might encounter some form of intelligent life, but I didn't think it would happen so quickly," Dr. Connors said.

"Perhaps not doctor, the absence of any signal from the rogue planet suggests there is no current activity there, but we may find what they were interested in," West said.

"West, do you have anything further?" Lionheart asked.

"Not at present Captain."

"Very well. I want a status report from all of you on your departments within the hour. If no one has anything, this meeting is adjourned," Lionheart said.

Later, Lionheart stood alone in his cabin with the lights out, looking out at the green nebula. He couldn't escape the dream he had where he felt someone was calling out to him. It was the last thing he expected to experience so far from Earth.

18. ALONE IN HIS CABIN, Lionheart looked out at the nebula. Its green, glowing gas makes him wonder about the voice calling him in his dream.

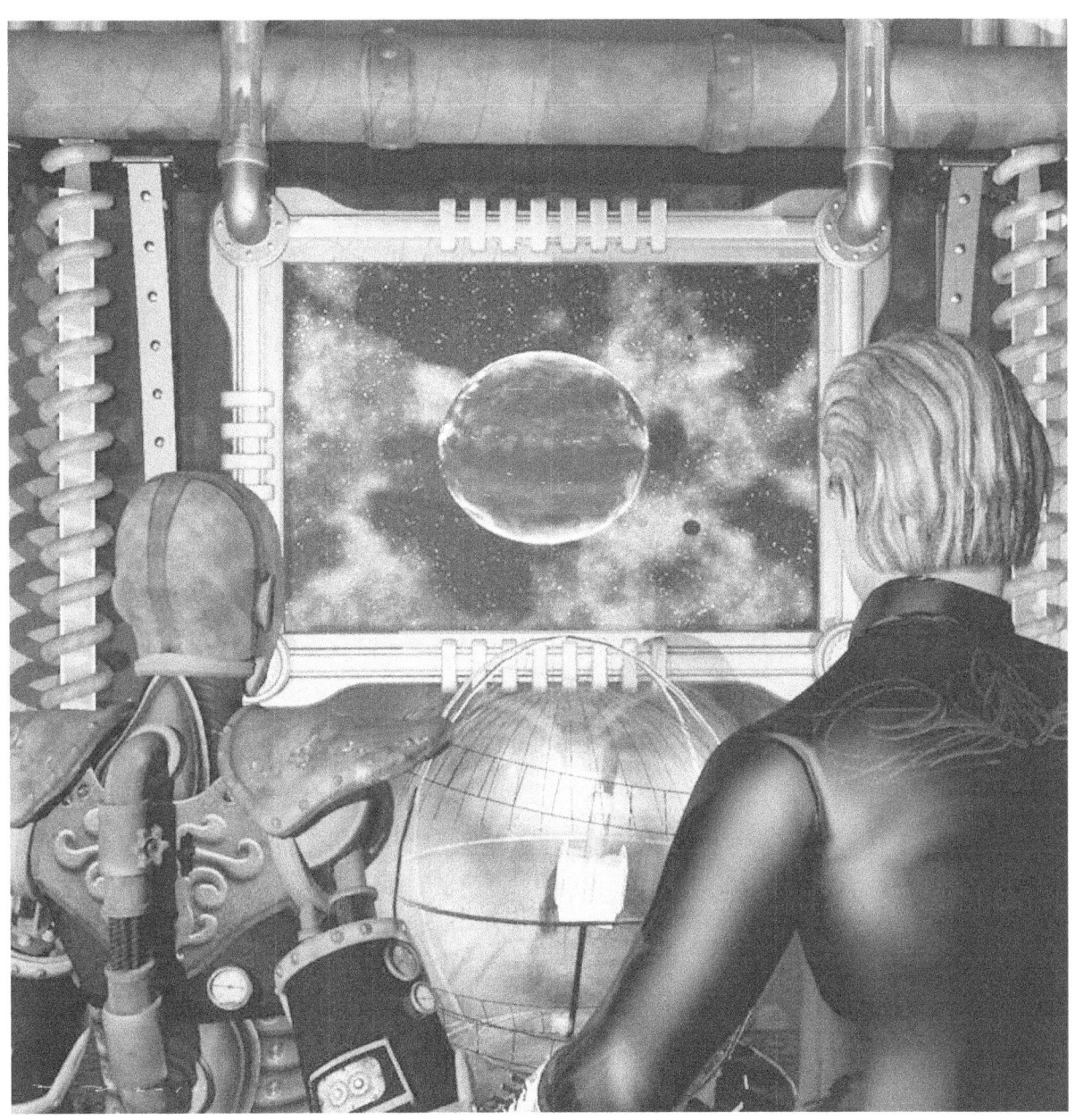

19. THE ROGUE PLANET almost had a ghostly appearance as the Onyx Tower approached from space. This was highlighted by the faint glow coming from its upper atmosphere.

Lionheart had the lights on the bridge dimmed to get a better view of this dark world. It was approximately the same size as Jupiter, and had several large moons, the largest of which was the approximate size of Mars. With only the illumination from starlight and the green nebula, the planet and it's moons were barely visible.

"What do you make of the glowing clouds?" Lionheart asked, looking out at the Jovian planet.

"Sensors have detected the presence of luciferin and an enzyme luciferase. This would suggest a possible form of bioluminescence in the planet's upper atmosphere, Captain," West said.

"Captain, I would like to have a sample collected," Connors said.

"Yes doctor. That can be arranged. Mr. Quinn set speed to match the winds of the planet's upper atmosphere. We'll drop in and collect a sample," Lionheart said.

"Aye sir" Quinn responded.

"This is the captain. We are about to drop into the upper atmosphere of the Jovian planet ahead. The ship will move at the planet's wind speed and direction; however, the gravity will be at approximately two point six so while we are there, position yourselves accordingly. The mechanical crew will still be active and carry out the task of collecting atmospheric samples. That is all, captain out," Lionheart said

A short time later, the Onyx tower briefly dropped into the Jovian planet's upper atmosphere, but once there, what they initially thought was a form of glowing microbial life proved far more elusive. To have calm surroundings, Lionheart had the tower match the 400 miles per hour wind speeds and direction. Up close, the millions of tiny glowing lights became a sort of optical illusion. Unable to collect any samples, Lionheart gave the order to return back into orbit. It was a good thing because while under 2.6 gravity, the living crew became somewhat uncomfortable.

20. **FOR A BRIEF TIME ONLY,** the Onyx Tower matched speed and direction of the winds in the upper atmosphere of the Jovian planet.

"Captain, ships sensors have detected a faint signal coming from the planets largest moon. They have also detected something unusual on the surface," West said.

"What is it?" Lionheart asked.

"There appears to be a large spherical object on the surface. Also, nearby there is an unusual rock like forest formation consisting of a black, stone like compound, sensors can't determine," West said.

"An unknown element?" Lionheart asked.

"Yes, at least in part. The formation has trace elements consistent with the surrounding area, but there is something else sensors can't identify."

"Interesting. Is there anything unusual about the sphere?" Lionheart asked.

"There are no power readings of any kind. Sensors indicate it is somewhat fragmented. If it is, or was a ship like the one we encountered, I suggest this could be a shipwreck of some kind," West answered.

"Well, let's have a closer look. Mr. Quinn set us down approximately five miles from the sphere. I will lead the landing party. West, Petrov and Ross will join me. Mr. Thornton, I want you to direct the ship's sensors at the other two stars in this trinary system and report when we return. You have the com," Lionheart commanded.

The Onyx Tower landed just behind a low ridge, approximately five miles from the sphere. With a height of 1200 feet [365.8 m], much of the sphere was still clearly visible from the tower. Two amphibians were dispatched. Lionheart and West were in one while Petrov and Ross were in the other. As they came up over the smooth ridge towards the sphere, Lionheart was somewhat overwhelmed by the sphere's size. Most of it was above ground. The bright lights of the amphibians did little to illuminate the sphere in the dim light of interstellar space. As they got closer, the base of the sphere in front of them became clearly visible. Only fragments of the sphere's outer skin remained, revealing what looked like a broken, burned out, skeletal interior. It

48

reminded Lionheart of a bombed-out building that was still standing. Approaching the base, he wondered about the possibility of the sphere collapsing down on them.

21. AFTER THE ONYX TOWER LANDED, the alien ship was clearly visible, even from miles away.

22. AS THEY GOT UP CLOSER, Lionheart and the others examined the skin of the alien ship.

It was clear that the sphere was the wreck of an alien starship. West surmised that it must have been related to the same spherical ship they encountered in space. Lionheart ordered Petrov to inspect the wreckage for any sign of the drive system, if any still existed. Deep scratches and gouges were clearly visible as Lionheart and West examined the outer hull.

"What the devil happened here. What could have caused this marking?" Lionheart asked.

"The damage to the outer hull is inconsistent with the surrounding terrain. If this ship crashed landed and rolled to a stop, the hull damage would be very different," West said.

"Possibly. However, it's possible the crash may have happened long ago when the terrain was different," Lionheart said.

"I don't think so. An analysis of the area revealed the rocks and boulders are mostly made of soft soil. There is nothing present that could account for these puncture holes and scratches. It had to be made by something different," West said.

"It almost looks like they could have been made by a pack of animals trying to claw their way in," Lionheart said.

"Interesting," West said as she examined one of the puncture holes closer with a hand-held scanning device. "There appears to be minute traces of something my instrument can't identify," she said holding the scanner closer. "Yes. Whatever this is, it appears to be the same substance the forest formation is made of. I'm going to collect a small sample, also, I'm picking up a faint signal," West said.

"What about the signal? Can you determine where it is coming from?" Lionheart asked.

"It seems to be coming from somewhere high up inside," West said holding the scanner up.

After West collected the hull sample, they made their way into the sphere's interior, through the wreckage. Lionheart was curious to see if there were any clues, such as a doorway or a chair that would give any indication of what the aliens might have been like physically. They found nothing. It was clear, whatever it was that caused the outside markings, got into the interior as well. Most everything appeared to be shredded by something very powerful. Lionheart's party was unable to reach the upper levels where the signal was coming from.

Lionheart never expected the first encounter with intelligent life to be a shipwreck, then again, the actual voyage so far was not at all what he imagined. After their examination, Lionheart sent small drones into the sphere to photograph and document as much of its remains as possible. The source of the signal came from a small inner sphere structure, located near the top of the wreckage. As interesting as exploring the alien ship was, Lionheart was anxious to move on to the dark forest formation they detected before landing. Before departing, the Onyx Tower would hover over the wreck while West and Petrov where lowered by a tether to make a closer inspection of the signal source.

A short time later, they arrived at the unusual forest like formation several miles away. Reaching the outer edge, Lionheart had the sensation it was a thick forest entirely composed of large, black, fruit trees. There were hundreds of them. Their pitch-black skin reflected almost no light, making them difficult to see clearly, even up close. As crewman Ross looked up at them, he had the sensation they were dark alien monsters under the light of the green nebula. Their sizes varied anywhere from five to fifty feet high. The tree's general form was that of a heavy stock that split off into smaller branches that arch outward with a bulb feature hanging at the ends. West was able to break off one of the smaller bulbs for a sample. When the sample broke it off, the break itself revealed a brittle material, similar to obsidian glass.

"Captain, as best I can determine at this point, the trees are composed of the exact same substance that was found on the sphere's hull," West said.

23. **AS CREWMAN ROSS LOOKED UP** at the tree like figures, he had the sensation they were dark alien monsters under the light of the green nebula.

"I know this may be a little far-fetched, but do you think it's possible that the sphere might have landed on a forest like this one? Long ago there might have been one around that location. I was thinking broken shards of this material might have caused those markings," Lionheart said.

"It's possible, but unlikely. If that were the case, the area around the sphere would have bits of that material all around its base. I may know more when we get this sample back to the ship's lab," West said.

When the landing parties returned to the Onyx Tower, Thornton had completed his report of the other two stars in the trinary system.

"Captain, I have the report on the other two stars you asked for," Thornton said.

"Very good. What did you find?"

"Both stars are very similar to our sun. The furthest star is 437 AU's distant from our current position. Around it, there are four Jovian planets, one of which is in the habitable zone. Interestingly enough, we have detected traces of oxygen. The nearest star is 121 AU's distant from us. We have detected seven planets around it. There appears to be a double planet system in the fourth orbit, just on the outer edge of the habitable zone. One of them appears to be Earth like, and the other, Mars like. The Earth like planet has a moon, and we have detected an unusual energy source coming from it, but we don't know what to make of it." Thornton reported.

"What do you mean?" Lionheart asked.

"Well, this moon appears to be collecting and focusing sunlight on the planet like a magnifying glass, but the level of sunlight the moon receives isn't great enough to produce the kind of beam emanating from it. And there's another thing. The planet's average surface temperature is 33.6°F [.87°C]. Without that energy beam coming from its moon, we estimate the planet's surface temperature would plunge down to -56.2°F [-49°C], because of its position at the outer edge the habitable zone.

"What about the Mars like planet?"

"We also detected something there that we can't explain. There are unusually high amounts of calcium in its atmosphere," Thornton reported.

"Calcium?" Lionheart asked with a puzzled look. He paused for a moment. "Good work Thornton. When we depart from here, the Mars like planet will be our next port of call. I think we have seen all of the obsidian forest we need to see. There is one more place we need to visit before leaving. Mr. Quinn. raise the tower and put us one hundred feet above the alien shipwreck and hold position," Lionheart commanded.

"Aye sir," Quinn responded.

In the light of the green nebula, the Onyx Tower had the appearance of a ghost castle as it hovered above the shipwreck.

"Captain, we have located the source of the signal. It's coming from a location just under the top of the sphere. West and Petrov are on the tether and ready to lower," Thornton said.

"All right, let's get a closer look. Lower away Thornton."

"Aye sir," Thornton responded.

As Petrov and West were lowered down through one of the openings in the top of the sphere, Petrov began to have a feeling of foreboding. Like mountain climbers being lowered into a rocky crevasse, they pushed off from the twisted metal interior as they slowly descended. Approximately forty feet below the surface, they came upon a small sphere like structure that looked to be wedged into the surrounding twisted wreckage. It was 12 feet [3.7m] in diameter. Like everything else around, it also had deep scratch marks, but it was unpenetrated. After several failed attempts to open its shell with a high energy gun, West and Petrov returned to the Tower. Lionheart and Dr. Connors met with them in the science lab.

"Analysis West?" Lionheart asked.

24. **IN THE LIGHT OF THE GREEN NEBULA,** the Onyx Tower had the appearance of a ghost castle as it hovered above the shipwreck.

"Not at this time Captain. Petrov and I were unable to penetrate the signal sphere (as we now call it). In spite of the scratches and gouges, there were no seams of any kind on its surface, no way to enter that we could find. Even though its surface had the appearance of a dull gray metal, it was actually highly reflective. When we tried to open it, our energy beam reflected away, cutting through metal around it. We stopped when Petrov and I realized we were cutting away at structural walls and floor supporting it," West said.

"Anything new about the signal?" Lionheart asked.

"All we know is that it keeps repeating itself. I'm still currently running several algorithms against it, in an attempt to (at least in part) determine its meaning. This may take some time," West said.

"Time is one thing we appear to have plenty of. Mr. Petrov, were you able to make any determination of what this shipwreck's propulsion system might have been?"

"No Captain. Inside the structure, there were only large open cavities where an engine room might have been, assuming they would even have one as we know it," Petrov said.

"He's right captain. Just after you got back, we got the results of the carbon dating analyses and according to it, that wreckage out there is over a hundred thousand years old. That being the case, studying its remains would be the equivalent of determining the detail of an ancient city with only a couple of stones to look at," Connors said.

"Well, considering what we discovered came from the remnants of the nebula, I'd say we are off to a good start. I think there is a good chance we'll discover more at the next solar system we visit. At least it is still intact. Mr. Petrov, since we will only be traveling a short distance of 121 AU's to our next destination, I need to create a very small space wave," Lionheart said.

"That will not be a problem, Captain. I'll need Mr. Thornton to assist me," Petrov said.

"I'll have him meet you in engineering," Lionheart said.

Cold Desert

The Onyx Tower departed from the rogue planet on a heading for the nearest star. After Petrov and Thornton adjusted the singularity devices necessary to create a miniature space wave, Lionheart gave the order. Less than an hour later, the Onyx Tower approached the double planet system in the fourth orbit. For a brief moment, Lionheart and the others on the bridge said nothing as they looked out at the second Earth like exoplanet they encountered. Looking over at West, Lionheart could see the blank expression on her face meant that she was receiving a lot of telemetry from the ship's sensors.

"Analysis West?" Lionheart asked.

"The larger Earth like planet (call it, planet "4A" if you will) has a mass of 1.2 that of Earth. The atmosphere closely matches the same ratio of oxygen nitrogen as Earth. Water to land mass ratio is also approximately the same as Earth except here, 73% of the land is concentrated into a single land mass, making it what would be described as a super continent. The smaller Mars like planet (call it planet "4B") is now 463,000 miles [745,127 km] away. It appears to be very Mars like in every respect, except it's surface temperature is much warmer than expected. Even though it has a thin atmosphere, small amounts of liquid water and plant life have been detected. It is most unusual," West said.

"What do you mean?" Thornton asked.

Like the larger planet, 4B also has a mostly oxygen nitrogen atmosphere with a slightly lower surface pressure than that of Earth. Considering the planet's mass and proximity to the sun, it should have almost no atmosphere at all. Its low gravity would not have been strong enough to keep it from being blown off by solar winds. The presence of plant life suggests the atmosphere provides some protection from the sun's harmful rays. Planet 4B is mostly a barren world, but the air is breathable. We have detected an area with a high concentration of unnatural features," West said.

"You mean manmade, possibly buildings?" Lionheart asked.

25. **THE MINI SPACE WAVE** produced by the Onyx Tower reduced the 121 AU travel time to only 47 minutes, 53 seconds. As the tower approached the double planet system in the fourth orbit, the Mars like planet was the first place of interest.

"Yes Captain, I believe the area was once the capital city of this world. The remains of other, much smaller settlements scattered all over this planet have also been detected," West said.

"Remains?" Thornton asked.

"Yes, the complete lack of activity and energy readings suggest whoever once lived here is gone. This planet was clearly inhabited. I am curious. There is something I can't explain," West said.

"What do you mean?" Lionheart asked.

"The plant life. I have reason to believe it may be the result of artificial life that was created in an attempt to terraform this planet," West said.

"Somehow, I've heard of a world like this before," Lionheart said quietly.

"Pardon me Captain?" West asked.

"Planet 4B, reminds me of what people once imagined Mars might be like. Long ago, there was a famous author who wrote several adventure stories that took place on Mars before we really knew anything about that planet," Lionheart said.

West looked away for a moment as she pulled the reference from the ship's library. "Yes, this author wrote ten adventure books in this series. His work inspired thousands, even long after his death."

"West, what can you tell me about planet 4A's moon?" Lionheart asked.

"It is similar to our own in size and surface soil composition, except it's surface appears to be very young and there are almost no craters. It orbits only 33,000 miles from planet 4A. Unlike Earth's moon, it's mass seems unusually low, suggesting that portions of its interior might be hallow. It also has an unusual rotation that I can't make sense of," West said.

"What do you mean?" Lionheart asked.

"It is rotating on its side, perpendicular to the planet. What makes it unusual is that, as the moon orbits, its spin axis remains pointed directly at planet 4A. Even though the moon is spinning, it also continues to keep the same side facing the planet. In the natural world, when a body rotates, the constant spin force away from the its axis keeps that axis pointing in the same direction. However, in the case of this moon, the spin axis always points toward the planets center. This in not natural. There must be a powerful unknown force acting on it. The moon is now passing on the far side of planet 4A. I'll know more when I have had a chance to study it further", West said.

"Captain, we are approaching planet 4B. We will be passing within a hundred miles of it shortly," helmsman Anders said.

"Mr. Anders, take us into an orbit around planet "4B". West, direct the ship's sensors to start mapping the planet. Let's get a closer look," Lionheart commanded.

"Aye sir. Orbital course laid in," Anders responded.

"I have already begun mapping Captain. This planet also appears to have an extensive network of canals. We are now passing into the planet's shadow," West reported.

"I wonder what kind of lights well see as we pass over to the dark side," Thornton said.

"I was wondering about that myself," Lionheart said.

"It's possible, but unlikely," West said.

As they all looked down at the planet's surface, there was only darkness. "I don't see anything, not even a campfire," Connors said.

"This is strange," Lionheart said quietly. "West, what is the rotation period of this planet?"

"It is 22 hours and 46 minutes, Captain," West replied.

26. **AS THEY STOOD AROUND THE WARDROOM'S LUMINARY TABLE,** West explained the unusual orbital rotation of Planet 4A's moon.

"We will hold in orbit until we have mapped the planet completely, then decide where the best place to land is. Mr. Thornton, you have the bridge. I'll be in my quarters," Lionheart said.

Lionheart found himself standing alone in the ruins of a small desert settlement. The only sound was the wind blowing through what was left of the deserted buildings. He stood at the end of main street. It was just after sunset and getting dark. The street ended at the base of a small hill, just beyond the town limits. A monument stood at top of it. The shadowed monument was almost impossible to discern. It was silhouetted by a green light behind it. Lionheart started walking down the street, toward it. Getting closer, he thought he could hear someone calling out to him. He was too far away to hear what the voice was saying. About halfway down the street, it became difficult to walk. Eventually, his feet became locked, and he could no longer move. The voice was much louder, but he still couldn't tell what it was saying. With a violent attempt to free his legs, Lionheart woke from another disturbing dream. Several hours had passed. As he sat up, he noticed his cabin was completely immersed in the soft light coming from the green nebula. Almost from the moment they returned to normal space, Lionheart had a sense of someone calling him. He also had a feeling of being watched. Looking out, he could see the sun rise as the ship came out from the dark side of planet 4B. His com sounded.

"Lionheart," he said.

"Captain, we have mapped planet 4B in detail," Thornton said.

"Very good. Have Connors, Holsten, Burkeman, West, and Ross meet me in the wardroom."

"Aye Captain."

Later, Lionheart met the others in the wardroom. "So, this is planet 4B," he said, as he looked down at the large closeup telemetry images laid out across the table. He noticed the faint web of geometric lines in a zig-zag pattern, running all across the planet. They were confirmed to be manmade canals. The ruins detected looked more like remains of ancient desert settlements on Earth. Looking closer at the images, Lionheart could see that a light stone material had been used for most everything man made, making it much easier to discern against the red desert landscape. "It looks like they used the same material for all their building construction," Lionheart said.

"As far as we can tell, everything is made of tridymite, Captain. Apparently, it is in abundance on this planet," West said.

"Tridymite? This planet must have been very volcanic at one time," Thornton said.

"I don't recall seeing a canal layout of this magnitude. It covers almost the entire planet. This network of canals reminds me of an old map of Mars, before it's surface could be seen close up. I'm no expert, but beyond the canals, some scattered ruins, and what looks like the only major city, I don't see any sign of the inhabitants," Connors said.

"As incredible as it may seem, this planet may very well be uninhabited. Aside from the buildings and canals, I don't see any sign of activity," Lionheart said, looking at one of the images through a magnifying glass.

"Does anyone have any idea where our first landing site should be?" Thornton asked.

"Captain, If I may, I would like to suggest somewhere in this area," West said, handing Lionheart one of the images.

Not saying anything at first, Lionheart studied the image. It was clear he couldn't make out what he was seeing. "What exactly am I looking at? This almost looks like a large man-made crater," he said, laying the image out on the table. The image showed an area where several canals converged at a single point, forming a lake in the middle of the only large city. In the center of the lake was an island. The island was dominated by a crater that had very steep walls, all around. There were buildings inside the crater, but the area was mostly open scorched land. Surrounding the crater was what looked like a deep burned out crevasse.

27. HAVING THE LARGE TELEMETRY IMAGES spread out in front of them, Lionheart and crew decide where the Tower will land on planet 4B.

"The deep ring around the crater wall looks like a giant fire pit," Thornton said.

"This island looks like it might have been the very heart of the only large city," Burkeman said.

"There is another reason why I suggested this site, Captain," West said.

"What is it?" Lionheart asked.

"Ships sensors have detected a high concentrate of calcium phosphate in the crater's soil. I believe it may hold a clue to the inhabitants of this planet," West said.

"If it is related to an organic process, the only way to tell is to get a soil sample," Connors said.

For a moment, Lionheart was quiet. Directly in front of him was an image of a small settlement that caught his attention. "Just a moment," he said as he held his magnifying glass over it. The settlement reminded him of the one he saw in his dream. At one end of it was a hill, and there was some kind of ruin on top of it.

"I agree, but before we set down in the capital city, I would like to make a more cautious approach. I want to get a closer look at a smaller settlement in an outlying area, like this one. There is something about this that peaks my curiosity," Lionheart said as he pointed to one of the images.

The Onyx Tower landed approximately a hundred miles south of the crater site, not far from the small settlement of interest. Lionheart had Peterson fly a rotor craft over the buildings to get first reconnaissance. There was no sign of anyone. It was clear the settlement had been deserted for a long time. An amphibian was launched, carrying Holsten, Connors, Ross, West and Lionheart. An echo of Lionheart's dream came back as the amphibian came to a stop at the end of the settlement's main street. At the far end of the street was a hill. Lionheart could see that there were some ruins just beyond the top of it, but he couldn't make them out. The street was actually a wide dirt road that was defined by the one and two-story building ruins on both sides. It reminded

Lionheart of an ancient desert city in the middle east. The cold air of planet 4B was breathable, but they had to adjust for the thinner air that was the equivalent an elevation of 9000 feet [2743.2m] on Earth. Walking through the settlement, they found scratches and punch marks on the walls of many buildings. They looked the same as those found earlier at the shipwreck site on the dark moon. An analysis done by West revealed they had traces of the same unknown obsidian material. As the landing party made their way through the settlement, all they could hear was the wind. Dr. Holsten had the feeling that the entire planet had been abandoned. The interiors of the buildings had been gutted, but they discovered some utensil fragments. It was clear that long term exposure had worn away any physical trace of what the inhabitants might have been like physically. That changed when Connors discovered a boot that was half buried in the soil.

"Something horrible happened here," she said as she held it up for the others to see.

"Lionheart was reminded of an old shipwreck that had been discovered at the bottom of the sea after a hundred years. The only thing related directly to the people that lost their lives were the remnants of leather shoes and boots.

"It would seem, whatever happened to the shipwreck we discovered earlier, also happened here. Except, what happened here seems fairly recent. I would guess anywhere between two to four centuries. I can't be more exact until I have made further study," West said, as she picked up another artifact to examine.

"I want to see what is at the top of the hill," Lionheart said as he started to walkup. When he reached the top, the ruins he wondered about came into full view. He was so overwhelmed by the site, he stopped and said nothing. One by one, the others from the landing party came up and stood next to him. They, too, were somewhat overwhelmed. Having completed her examination of an artifact, West came up the hill.

"Fascinating. It would seem there are other branches of humanity, light years away from Earth," West said.

28. "SOMETHING HORRIBLE HAPPENED HERE," Connors said, as she held it up the remains of a shredded boot for the others to see.

"I imagine this is what it must have been like, thousands of years ago, when primitive tribes encountered each other for the first time," Holsten said.

"Yes, only now we have encountered the remains of another tribe, nearly a thousand light years away from our little island," Lionheart said. In front of them was the partial remains of a human head carved from stone. It stood nearly twenty feet high. Most of it was gone, but what remained of the face was clearly human.

"Captain, Thornton here," came a voice from Lionheart's communicator.

"Lionheart here. What is it Thornton?"

"Captain, planet 4A's moon has come out from the dark side of the planet. We have detected what appears to be a high concentration of luminous energy emanating from the side of the moon that faces the planet. We have confirmed that it is a focused beam of concentrated sunlight,"

Lionheart and the others looked up at planet 4A in the sky above. Its moon was passing in front of it, but instead of casting a shadow, there was a bright spot in the clouds.

"What is that? What is happening?" crewman Ross asked.

"That moon is projecting a focused beam of sunlight light. We briefly detected it when we first entered this system," Lionheart said quietly.

"Captain, if the former inhabitants created what we are seeing, they were obviously highly advanced. It would also seem they have perfected an extreme power source. It's hard to believe that a race this advanced would have become extinct. There may be some still living on the planet 4A," West said.

"We will get there soon enough, but first I want to get a closer look at that island crater we spotted earlier," Lionheart said.

29. **THE LANDING PARTY FINDS EVIDENCE** of humans nearly a thousand light years from Earth.

Having concluded their investigation, they headed back to the Onyx Tower. In spite of the fantastic discovery of finding the remains of a civilization on a faraway planet, everyone was somewhat overwhelmed by the fact that there was no one still around. Shortly later, the tower landed on the island, just outside the crater. The ships head geologist, Dr. Bascom, wanted to have a closer look at the layer of crystalline material on the crater's outer wall.

Captain's Log: Our voyage elapsed time is now 101 days (Oct 3rd, 1627, Earth Time) The exploration of planet 4B continues. We landed at our second place of interest, an island in the middle of a capital city. It is dominated by a large crater (approximately 7 miles across). We later confirmed it was manmade. At the insistence of Dr. Bascom, the ship's head geologist, the first area we explored was outside the crater to examine its outer crystalline walls. We were unable to make any direct contact with the crystalline material, as even the smallest of pieces could easily cut thru our gloves, even the soles of our boots. Dr. Bascom was able to examine a small shard of the material under the ship's electron microscope. It turns out that this crystalline material has no discernible flat surface. It is essentially a solid consisting entirely of sharp spikes, pointing out in all directions. West believes the crystalline wall was created to keep any unwanted visitors (of any size and weight) from reaching the crater's interior. If anything, or anyone attempted to climb the outer wall, they would simply sink of their own weight into the crystalline material and die. In time, even their remains would sink further in and break down into even smaller fragments until nothing larger than a molecule remained. At that point, the rain and wind would remove the rest.

The outer wall of the crater is clearly the best example of ground defense engineering I have ever encountered. After our examination, we came to the conclusion that the crater is (or was) the site of some kind of grand fortress. This was later confirmed when we set down inside the crater itself. The buildings had the same scratches and puncture marks as we found elsewhere. We believe this was the last stronghold for whoever lived here. We believe the crystalline wall was built to keep out whatever was destroying the rest of the planet. However, in spite of that, whatever was out there, somehow got in. Vast amounts of bone fragments were discovered in the soil. This turned out to be the source of the calcium phosphate we detected earlier from space.

The bone fragments also revealed another interesting fact. According to Dr. Connors preliminary report, the DNA in the bone fragments are human with only slight variation. If this is indeed the case, it will fuel the idea that humans may not have originated on Earth. But for now, God only knows. So far, the discovery of planet 4B and the remains of its civilization has left everyone a little uneasy. For many, it's like the discovery of a brutal murder scene, and the haunting thought that the killer might still be around.

We are now moving on to our next destination of interest, planet 4A's moon. This moon may very well be the most unusual body we have encountered. As discovered earlier, its rotation defies the laws of physics. If the Earth's moon rotated in such a manner, it would be like watching the same face of our moon spin around like a wheel as it crossed the sky. Unlike the Earth's moon, this one orbits once every 10 hours and 23 minutes. At only 33,000 miles away, it's circular orbit is much closer to planet "4A" then the moon to the Earth, yet in spite of its close proximity, the gravitational tidal effects are minimal because it has an unusually low mass. West has concluded that much of its interior may be hollow.

Peter M. Lionheart, Captain

Crystal Engine

Sitting alone in his cabin, Lionheart looked out at the earth like planet and its moon. The Onyx Tower would arrive there in a few hours. After the brief exploration of planet 4B, Lionheart wasn't aware that he had gone for some time without rest. Without realizing it he fell asleep.

"Captain, Thornton here. Captain?"

"Lionheart here," Lionheart said in a groggy voice as he woke up.

"Sir, you wanted to be notified when we reached moon orbit," Thornton said.

"Very good Thornton," Lionheart responded.

"What do we have so far?" Lionheart asked as he came on the bridge a short time later.

"The moon is now passing over to the dark side of planet 4A and will emerge from its shadow in just under four hours from now," West said, as Lionheart looked out over the moon's dark surface. It was hard to discern any land features in the dim light of the green nebula.

"Captain, we have a preliminary map of this moon," West said as she motioned Lionheart to step back into the Wardroom. Hovering above the luminary table in the center of the room was a semi-transparent 3D electronic image. Most of the moon's surface consisted of smooth, rolling land with very few craters, that is, except for two. They were very deep, and each had what looked like a glass floor, well below the rim of the outer wall. In some respects, they were not like craters at all, because each had several deep canyons extending out from the center. The two craters were located on exact opposite sides of the moon, and their size and shape looked almost identical. They were located directly on the moon's rotation axis.

As Lionheart looked at the 3D image, he noticed an enlarged likeness of the Onyx Tower approaching the outer pole of the moon.

"Mr. Thornton. Slow the ship. Take us out of orbit and bring us to a hover above the moon's outer pole. Set altitude for ten miles and hold position. I want to get a better look at it," Lionheart commanded.

"Aye sir," Thornton responded.

A short time later, the Onyx Tower came to a hover directly above the moon's outer pole. The green light of the nebula gave the tower a ghostly appearance as it hovered above. The main opening of the crater below was approximately 12 miles [19.3 km] across. The deep canyon tributaries extended outward at an average distance of at least 30 miles [48.3 km] from the center. The glass like floor of the crater was highly reflective. It's reflection of the stars and nebula gave the crew the impression the moon was hollow. Lionheart and the others became quiet as they looked down into the grand crater below. Mrs. West became very quiet with a distant look on her face. Lionheart could tell she was receiving and processing massive amounts of telemetry from the ships sensors.

"Captain, sensors have detected most of the crater's floor is covered with the same crystalline material found on planet 4B. Contrary to the crater's dormant appearance below, sensors have detected a high energy field just below the surface. The field's effect in the surrounding terrain below is clearly visible in infrared," West said as she switched the main viewing screen on the bridge.

"My God," Lionheart said as he tried to comprehend exactly what he was looking at. Everyone on the bridge became quiet.

In the live inferred image, the floor of the crater looked like clear transparent glass with a faint web-like frame running through it. Below the floor was a grand shaft opening that extended deep into moon's interior. Near the base of the shaft, the walls began to have an orange glow. Beyond the bottom of the shaft, the orange glowing ground appeared to be rotating in the direction opposite the moon's rotation.

"Ship sensors indicate the shaft that you're looking at is just over ten miles wide. The rotating ground surface is 43 miles [69.2 km] deep. This moon has almost no atmosphere. There is something else. I can't make it out. It is some sort of unusual background noise. I'm having the ship's sensors wash the static," West said.

30. THE ONYX TOWER CAME TO HOVER directly above the moon's outer pole. The green light of the nebula gave the tower a ghostly appearance as it hovered above. Planet 4B was visible on the crater's reflective surface.

"Is it my imagination or does the crater floor look like a gigantic stained-glass window with some of the pieces missing here and there," Thornton said, with his mouth hanging open.

"That would be an accurate observation Mr. Thornton," West said.

"Some of those openings look large enough for the ship to pass through," Lionheart said.

"Most all of them are Captain. Even though they appear relatively small from our vantage point, they average anywhere between one to seven hundred meters across. Wait. Just a moment. Just a moment," West said, lifting her hand as though she was straining to hear something.

"Yes. Captain ship sensors have detected a very faint signal emanating from deep in the moon's interior. I can't make out any specific location. There is too much interference," West said.

"We have to find the source of that signal. Mr. Petrov...".

"Aye Captain," Petrov responded on the com.

"Launch a probe into the crater. I want a live telemetry feed in the Wardroom," Lionheart commanded.

"Aye Sir," Petrov responded.

A moment later, Lionheart, West, Thornton and Bascom were in the Wardroom. A transparent 3D image of the crater was projected on the wardroom's luminary table. As they watched, a tiny point of light (representing the probe) was dropped from the tower. It carefully maneuvered through one of the openings as it passed thru the glass floor of the crater. As it made its way further down, the 3D image projection changed to show the probe's surroundings. When it reached the bottom of the shaft, the walls all around opened up too wide for the probe to detect. The image of everything around the probe disappeared until it reached the bottom. The probe was now 43 miles [69.2 km] in the moon's interior, hovering just above the center of the rotating ground below.

"The probe's sensitivity is too low to detect any of its surroundings clearly. I'm going to increase sensitivity to maximum. This should allow us to see much further away," West said.

As the probe sensitivity increased, the cavern ceiling near the shaft above became visible.

"According to the probe, the surrounding cavern has an average ceiling height of approximately five miles [eight km]. A cavern of this magnitude is not unusual, considering the moon's extremely low gravity," West said.

"The probe's sensor range seems limited. I would like to see more of its surroundings. Is there any way to increase its sensitivity?" Lionheart asked.

"Probe sensors are already a maximum, Captain. Strong magnetic interference is blocking sensor range," West said.

"Do you have anything further on the signal?" Lionheart asked.

"There is still a great deal of interference caused by the surrounding energy field, but it appears to be coming from somewhere along the moon's equator," West said.

"Captain, we may be able to, at least in part, pinpoint the signal source by having the probe fly around the shaft opening in a circular pattern, slowly spiraling outward with each pass," Thornton suggested.

"Mr. Petrov, have the probe hold at two miles [3.2 km] above the cavern floor, then plot a circular course that takes it a little further away from the shaft's center axis with each pass. Let's see how large this cavern is," Lionheart said.

"Aye Sir," Petrov responded.

The probe began to move sideways into the surrounding cavern. As everyone watched, more of the cavern's ceiling and floor became visible as the probe moved away from the shaft entrance. After circling the center axis point eleven times and reaching a distance of seven miles away, the 3D image began to break up.

"What is happening?" Thornton asked.

"Interference from the energy field is breaking up the signal," West said.

As they watched, the probe began to violently wobble up and down. Then it flew into the cavern's ceiling and the 3d image vanished.

"West?" Lionheart asked.

"As the probe flew into the cavern, the surrounding magnetic fields became too intense for it to go any further. It did not have the power necessary to maintain stability. After struggling against two opposing fields, the probe finally succumbed to one and crashed, in this case the ceiling. But, before it crashed, we were able to get a location on that signal. It's coming from the equator. There is something else. Did anyone notice that there was no change in the ceiling and floor as the probe flew further into the surrounding cavern? Even though it wasn't noticeable in the 3D image, probe telemetry indicates both the floor and ceiling are spherical, one inside the other. It would seem the entire outer surface of this moon is actually a hollow sphere, with another sphere inside it that is rotating in the opposite direction. Given the fact that both the floor and ceiling of the cavern are covered with a highly conductive crystalline material, the outer and inner moon are configured much like an electric generator, one that is producing power on an unprecedented scale," West said, as she projected a 3D model to make her point.

31. **THE PROBE LAUNCHED INTO THE MOON'S INTERIOR** revealed that it was actually hollow, with another moon inside.

"This is fantastic," Lionheart said quietly. "Mrs. West, could the Onyx Tower withstand the influence of these fields if it were down inside the moon where the probe was?"

"Yes, as long as the fields stay at their current levels," West replied.

"Captain, what are you thinking?" Thornton asked.

"I would like to find the source of that signal and have a closer look at this lunar engine. Mr. Petrov, what is the status of ship's shields?" Lionheart asked.

"All systems are fully operational at one hundred percent, Captain," Petrov responded through the com.

"I want a closer look. Mr. Quinn plot a course to the location of that signal on the equator," Lionheart commanded.

"Aye Captain," Quinn responded.

"Captain, I have a bad feeling about this. I find the thought of flying this ship underground very unsettling," Thornton said.

"Duly noted Mr. Thornton. If we can handle a direct hit from a uranium bomb, I think we can handle whatever we find below. After we find the source of that signal, I plan to fly the ship on to the inner pole. If my guess is correct, the forces at work inside this moon are so powerful, everything will be held securely in its place," Lionheart said.

"You mean it's very unlikely the inner wall of the outer moon will not collide with the outer wall of the inner moon, crushing us in an instant," Thornton said.

"Will, that's one way to put it," Lionheart said laughing.

"Course laid in sir," Quinn responded.

"Very Good, Mr. Quinn. Take us down slow and have the ship hover when we have reached the halfway point between the outer and inner moon," Lionheart commanded.

32. **THE REFLECTIVE GLASS FLOOR** of the crater had the appearance of a mirror as the Onyx Tower descended towards the moon's interior.

The Onyx Tower slowly descended into the outer pole's crater. Moments later, it passed through the opening in the crater floor and entered the shaft. Soon after, the tower looked as if it were descending in total darkness. Aside from the ships lights, the only other source of light came from the stars and nebula in the shaft opening above, and it was getting smaller. The main view screen (still showing infrared) on the bridge revealed a different view. It looked as though they were descending into a glowing lava volcano. The tower came to a stop, hovering two and a half miles [four km] above the cavern floor.

"We have reached the halfway point between the outer and inner moon and are directly above the axis of the outer pole Captain," Quinn said.

"Very good Mr. Quinn. Mr. Petrov?"

"Petrov here."

"What percentage of shield power is needed to counter the surrounding energy field?" Lionheart asked.

"Only 16% sir," Petrov responded.

"Very good. Set shield intensity to match surrounding energy fields and adjust as required."

"Aye sir."

"Mr. Quinn, take us to the signal source on the equator. Adjust course to coincide with the inner moon's rotation. Ahead slow, set speed for arrival in one hour," Lionheart commanded.

The ship began to move sideways. The tower was almost in total darkness. Occasionally, there were silent, snake like, streaks of lightning moving across the crystalline surfaces above and below. They emanated from the outer pole. Flashing past, they illuminated the surrounding crystals. Some of them were so bright, even the tower and it's energy shield became visible.

"I never imagined anything like this," Lionheart said quietly.

33. THE MOON'S INTERIOR was actually a gigantic electromagnetic engine, capable of producing power on colossal scale.

As they traveled along, West had activated the 3D imager in the Wardroom. It was clear they were moving between an outer and inner moon. Magnetic fields began to increase dramatically as they approached the equator. The flashes of lightning that moved through the crystals above and below were becoming more frequent. They now were moving in a constant direction, approximately 45 degrees off the straight-line course the tower was following.

"The magnetic fields are fluctuating. There has been a sudden rise in their field strength, Captain. The lines of force appear to be shifting the moon's rotation axis, keeping it pointed at the center of planet 4A. We should reach the equator in seven minutes. Also, the signal is becoming intermittent. One minute it's there, the next, it's not," West said.

"So, this is why the moon's rotation axis keeps adjusting to point to the center of the planet", Thornton said.

"Mr. Petrov, how are the shields holding up?" Lionheart asked.

"They are at 65% and rising sir. Captain at this rate, there is a chance they will exceed 100% just before we reach the equator. Captain, if that happens…".

"Understood Mr. Petrov. Keep me updated," Lionheart said interrupting.

At five miles from the equator, lightning began to jump across the moon's interior, often striking the Onyx Tower. As it did, the tower's magnetic shields became more luminous. The strikes were becoming more intense and frequent.

"Captain, shields are now at 87%," Petrov reported.

"Sir, we will cross the equator in two minutes," Quinn said.

"Maintain steady course Mr. Quinn. West are you still receiving the signal?" Lionheart asked.

"It's coming from just ahead of us, down on the surface of the inner moon," West responded.

"Captain, shields are now at "93%," Petrov said.

34. **AT FIVE MILES FROM THE EQUATOR,** lightning began to jump across the moon's interior, often striking the Onyx Tower. As it did, the tower's magnetic shields became luminous. The strikes became more intense and frequent.

"One minute to equator, Captain", Quinn reported.

"95%, Captain," Petrov reported with a raised voice.

"30 seconds," Quinn said.

"97%".

"15 seconds".

"98%".

"10 seconds".

"Captain were at 99%! If we pass 100 the tower could be destroyed," Petrov said in a frantic voice.

"5 seconds"

"99.7!"

"Crossing the equator now, Captain," Quinn said.

"Captain, the location of the signal has changed. It's coming from somewhere inside the ship!" West said.

Petrov became silent.

"Petrov?" Lionheart asked.

"97% and falling, Captain".

"Captain, the signal is gone. There is no trace of it sir. It is gone completely," West said.

"Gone completely?" Lionheart asked.

"Yes sir. Just as we passed over the equator, the source of the signal suddenly changed from the surface of the inner moon to somewhere in the lower levels of the ship. I have no explanation of the event. I'm running analysis now to see if I can determine exactly where the signal on the ship emanated from," West said.

"Do you think we can reacquire it if we go back?" Lionheart asked.

"I would strongly advise against it Captain. The signal is gone and if our magnetic shields fail..." West said, stopping herself.

"West is right Captain. Some of our shields burned out when we passed over the equator. We are down to 63% capacity. It will take several hours to repair," Petrov reported.

"Understood. Mr. Quinn, plot a course for the inner pole. We we'll exit from the opposite side we came in on," Lionheart commanded.

As the ship continued moving away from the equator, the lighting strikes became less frequent.

"We seem to be moving out of danger," Thornton said, taking a deep breath.

The moon came out from behind the shadow of planet 4A. The moon's inner pole was suddenly thrust into full sunlight. With the coming of sunlight in its shaft, the crystalline walls came alive with flashes of intense lightning. The sunlight had triggered a powerful energy storm. Moments later, it expanded down the polar shaft of the moon's inner pole. Then it began to move outward, towards the equator. It's outer boundary literally became a ten-mile-high tsunami of lightning filled, exploding fire.

"Captain, sensors indicate a massive power field is forming ahead. It seems to be emanating from the inner pole," West said with a sound of warning in her voice.

"All stop. Any idea what is causing it West?" Lionheart asked.

"The moon is passing out from planet 4A's shadow. I suspect the power field ahead is a reaction to the inner pole's exposure to direct sunlight," West said.

"So, we are stuck here. We can't go ahead and with our shields reduced, and we can't go back. I don't think this can get any worse," Thornton said.

35. **AS THE MOON CAME OUT FROM BEHIND THE SHADOW** of planet 4A, it's inner pole was suddenly thrust into full sunlight.

"Sensors indicate it is getting worse. The boundary of the energy field ahead will reach us in two minutes, thirty-seven seconds, and behind us, the equator's energy field is increasing. It will reach us in four minutes, seven seconds. Curious, its polarity has changed to match the polarity of the incoming field ahead," West said with an expressionless face, as she looked at Thornton.

"It may be only a few seconds, but I have to buy as much time as I can. Mr. Quinn, move the tower to the halfway point between the pole and the equator. We have to stay between the two energy fields for as long as we can," Lionheart commanded.

"Aye sir," Quinn responded.

"Captain, we can't handle another storm," Petrov said.

"Petrov, set our shield polarity to match. If my guess is correct, we won't have to," Lionheart said.

Moments later, the tower was at the mid-way point between the two energy storms. The horizons on opposite sides of the tower began to get lighter.

"Here it comes!" Thornton yelled.

"West, time to impact?" Lionheart asked.

"Seven seconds," West responded.

Just at that moment both walls of lightning appeared, each closing in from opposite sides of the ship.

"Six seconds- Five seconds-," West continued.

"What is happening?" Thornton asked.

"Look the storms are slowing!" Quinn yelled.

"Yes, just as I thought," Lionheart said quietly.

"Storms have stopped and are holding position Captain," West said.

"Like a small lion tamer caught helpless between two ferocious herds of angry lions, the Onyx Tower continued to hover. In the engine room, Petrov continued to sweat as the tower's shields held against the opposing storm fields. His instruments showed the shields were at 62.7%. If it went above 63% the tower would be crushed instantly. Lionheart began to rub his chain as he watched from the bridge. Shadows began to fall on the inner pole as the moon continued keep the same face toward planet 4A. The sun was no longer shining directly into the polar canyon. As the inner crater began to fall into shadow, the energy produced by direct sunlight began to diminish.

"There- That's it! It is just as I thought!" Lionheart said with excitement as he noticed the walls of the storms slowly beginning to recede.

West continued to sit quietly as she processed the latest telemetry from the ship. "Yes, both storms are starting to recede. Captain, how did you know?" West asked.

"It was just a best guess. When this moon was first observed, I notice that the beam of sun energy emanated only from its inner pole. We knew both energy storms had the same polarity, so that once they got in close proximity, they would repel from one another. Whoever created this moon's interior did so in such a way to allow energy to flow in only one direction, towards planet 4A. I think the builders also didn't want this moon's excess energy to bleed off into space, possibly effecting planet 4B. West, what is the status of the polar storm?" Lionheart asked.

"It is continuing to recede. At this rate, it will dissipate completely in 47 minutes. The equatorial storm is also receding," West said.

A great relief came over Petrov as the surrounding energy levels fell to levels the tower's shields could easily block.

"Mr. Quinn, continue on course toward the inner pole, keeping a safe distance from the storm as it dissipates," Lionheart Commanded.

36. **LIKE A SMALL LION TAMER** caught helpless between two ferocious herds of angry lions, the Onyx Tower held position between the two opposing energy storms.

The dawn of a new day was coming to the crater of the outer pole, as the surrounding mountain tops came into full sunlight. Moments later, as the sunlight eventually reached the canyon floor, gigantic bolts of lightning began to energize the walls of the polar shaft. With the coming of sunlight, there were only a few lightning bolts at first. Soon, what was only ten bolts became a hundred. Then a hundred became a thousand, and a thousand became a hundred thousand. Starting from the top of the polar shaft, they raced downward forming a grand spiral of storming light and energy. As it reached the inner moon, it was joined by a second wave of cloud like energy that emanated from its surface. With ever increasing power and no place to go, the storm pushed outward in all directions, heading to the equator. The outer pole was now coming into the light of mid-morning, which greatly increased the polar storms power. Minutes later, when it reached the equator, the polar storms energy wave was joined by a second energy storm. This time the equators storm merged with the polar storm as it passed over. The combined storms were now moving on to the inner pole with unstoppable energy.

"Captain, the storm ahead of us has dissipated completely. It is now safe to pass through the inner pole," Quinn Reported.

"Very good Mr. Quinn. What is the distance to the inner pole?" Lionheart asked.

"12 miles [19.3 km] sir. At our current speed, we will reach it in three minutes," Quinn responded.

"Captain, sensors had detected another energy storm sir. This one is a hundred times stronger and will be on our position in 43 seconds," West said.

"Mr. Quinn, get us out of here. Best speed", Lionheart commanded.

"I'll try Captain. We can outrun the storm. I'm worried about slowing down enough to turn the ship to make it out of the polar shaft," Quinn said as he started to increase speed.

With the exception of West, everyone became nervous as the tower increased speed. It wasn't long until the aft horizon began to light up, only this time it was much brighter. It was as though the inner moon was beginning to transform itself into a bright star. Even at reduced strength, the Onyx Tower's shields were strong enough to shatter the glass floor as it exited from the inner pole's crater. Once in space, it quickly flew off to one side to avoid the moon's focused sun rays. A moment later, the tower was far enough away to allow the whole moon to come into view. A great sense of relief came over Lionheart and the living crew. Showing no emotion, West and the rest of the mechanical crew had already calculated a stable trajectory from the path of the moon's energy beam.

Captain's Log: Our voyage elapsed time is now 103 days (Oct 5th, 1627, Earth Time) Even though we were on (or perhaps I should say in) planet 4A's moon for only the better part of a day, it feels like it's been a lifetime. In an odd way, I feel as though I have lunged far forward into the future. I have heard fantasy stories of civilizations that accomplished engineering on a planetary scale, but never envisioned it until now. I still can't help but wonder about what happened to the builders. Are any of them still around?

The "Moon Belt" (as we have come to call it) defines the equatorial region of planet 4A that is directly affected by the moon's energy beam as it passes overhead. The intense light (coming from the moon's inner pole) heats the belt area to an average temperature of 317°F [158.3°C]. After the moon has passed, the belt area cools down to an average of 156°F [68.8°C]. The moon belt is actually an area extending out from the equator by a hundred miles [161 kilometers], both north and south, making the belt two hundred miles [322 km] wide. Conditions in the belt are too harsh for most life, however without it, planet 4A would become a frozen wasteland.

I'm still haunted by the signal that lead us into the moon's interior. To my surprise and shock, West was able to later authenticate my voice coming from it. I'm completely baffled. Where did this message come from, or perhaps the real question is when? When this voyage began, West told me I was on a path. Is it possible part of my future passes through another time, into the present? It has before. Also, how is it possible that a signal came from the tower as we passed over the equator? I have West working on an explanation, but so far, she is as puzzled as I am.

Our next and final stop in this mini planetary system on the 4th orbit is planet "4A", or what we now refer to as "Pangaea". It was so christened because over 93% of the landmass is concentrated on a single continent. It is divided world because the moon belt runs across its entire equator. Pangaea's water to land ratio is approximately the same as Earth, and like the Earth, it is teaming with life. Preliminary observation has revealed a variety of plant and animal life that appears to have elements ranging from today's Quaternary period all the way back to the Jurassic period. As expected, no sign of any surface civilization has been discovered. I can only wonder if anyone was here, they must have suffered the same fate as planet 4B.

However, we did discover six points of interest. The first appears to be the entrance to an unusually large underground network of caverns. Before losing contact with our probe, it sent back images of what looked like unnatural features deep in the caves. West believed contact was lost due to interference from ground minerals throughout the area. The five other areas are of interest, because of two things they have on common in spite of their surrounding climate conditions. All of them appear to be completely unremarkable. They also appear to be in a slight shadow of some kind even though there is nothing above to cast a shadow. The shadow is so faint that only West was able to detect it. And lastly, the temperature in all of the them is a constant 72°F [22.2°C] while temperatures in the surrounding areas vary.

Large amounts of the unidentified element we came across on Planet 4B and the dark moon encountered earlier have been detected in planet 4A's upper atmosphere. Here it exists in the form of thousands upon thousands of small, black, floating globules that are being blown all across the planet by high winds. Mrs. West believes they are actually balloons that contain some kind of lighter-than-air gas. The most unusual thing about them is their flight pattern. They move along in what might be described as a black cloud that measures up to ten miles [16 km] across. The cloud moves along a spiral course that takes it from one pole to the other on an average of four days. It is almost as though the cloud was circling the planet looking for something.

P. M. Lionheart: Captain

37. **AFTER PASSAGE THROUGH THE INTERIOR** of planet 4A's moon, the Onyx Tower headed for planet 4A. **Top:** With maximum acceleration the Onyx Tower was able to exit the moon's inner pole before being incinerated by the moon's energy beam. **Bottom:** Upon reaching planet 4A, the tower's crew began searching for the best place to land and explore.

The Island

"Well, does anyone have a preference on what our first landing site should be?" Lionheart asked, as he addressed his officers in the wardroom.

"After talking it over, we feel the caverns where we lost contact with our probe would be a good place to start, Captain," Thornton said.

"Captain, our general consensus is that the caverns are the most likely place to hold the clues to what happened on planet 4B. They might also explain why this world seems to be devoid of any civilization in spite of having an un-natural moon," West said.

"Agreed, I'm anxious to have a closer look at what is down there. We'll set the tower down as close as we can to the entrance and launch a scout to survey the area. I want two landing parties. Dr. Holsten will head the science team. Mr. Thornton, I want you to lead both parties and take Ross with you," Lionheart commanded.

"Captain, if I may...," Dr. Connors said, interrupting.

"Yes Doctor, what is it?"

"I know we have surveyed the planet in great detail, but I would like to know more about the unknown element cloud that is in the atmosphere before we send anyone down there," Connors said.

"What would you suggest?" Lionheart asked.

"I would like to launch a probe into the cloud to collect a small sample," Connors said.

"I'm also curious about that material. West, what is the current location of the cloud?" Lionheart asked.

"It is currently moving toward the south pole and will arrive there approximately four hours from now, Captain," West said.

"Captain? I also have a place of interest I would like to pursue, or perhaps I should say, an island," Burkeman said, raising his hand.

"Yes Burkeman, what is it about this island that interests you?" Lionheart asked.

"It is a remote barren island in the northern hemisphere. The nearest land mass is over a thousand miles away. What interests me is what I discovered on some of the high-resolution images taken," Burkeman said, as he laid them out on the table in front of everyone. "If you look closely, you can see hundreds of tracks made by large animals. The tracks suggest they are possibly the size of elephants, yet the images show no sign of any animals on the island at all. I'm curious to find out how they got there. Right now, the tower's orbit will be taking us over the island, 27 minutes from now. I would like to dispatch a science team in two rotor crafts to investigate," Burkeman said.

"I take it you have already chosen your team?" Lionheart asked.

"Yes sir, they are in the rotor craft bays awaiting my orders," Burkeman said.

Lionheart got a faint smile on his face, then turned to Connors. "Dr. Connors, have we detected any kind of biological anomaly that might be considered potentially dangerous?" Lionheart asked.

"Only the cloud that is currently in the southern hemisphere, Captain," Connors responded.

"Who is on your team Burkeman?" Lionheart asked.

"Peterson and Skippers will pilot the two Rotorcrafts. I chose life sciences doctor's Breston and Dorian. Also, Mullin is coming along just in case we run into something unexpected," Burkeman said.

I think once anyone gets down there, the unexpected is probably the only thing we can expect. Very well Burkeman. Mr. Thornton slow the tower and take us down to twenty thousand feet over the island. We'll launch Burkeman's science team. After returning to space, alter course to take us into a polar orbit. When we are close enough, we'll launch a probe into the upper atmosphere and collect a sample of that black cloud," Lionheart commanded.

When the tower was over the island, two rotorcraft launched from their launch bays. As Peterson looked up, he could see the tower rising back up into space. At this altitude, there was almost no air for the rotor blades to grab on to. They would have to free fall until they reached the lower atmosphere. As Burkeman's science team looked out, they all felt they were back on Earth, somewhere in the south pacific. However, as they got lower, they could see that the island was surrounded by what looked like a belt of thick marshland that separated it from the surrounding ocean. Beyond the marshland was an underwater forest of green and orange vines. Peterson wondered if it was anything like the kelp forests of America's west coast. The inner part of the island was exactly as the images depicted, mostly flat and barren with an outcrop of hills at its center. It also had small natural jetties, extending outward into the marsh in all directions. Their length measured anywhere from two hundred yards up to a mile. The island itself was approximately twelve miles [19.3 km] in diameter. It was later referred to as Star Island because of its appearance from high altitude.

The air was now becoming thick enough for the rotors to work better. The two rotorcrafts were now flying around each other, forming a double helix vaper trail as they descended. At eight thousand feet up, they both flared out of the spiral and began to fly around the island. A closer look revealed that one of the hills at the island's center was not natural. It was a smooth half dome that had four large entrances evenly spaced around it. Peterson wondered if it might be some kind of temple. After circling the island, they both landed on a flat sandy beach on the south side. There was a slight breeze with what sounded like a combination of crickets and bull frogs coming from the marsh. Armed with a lightning gun, Mullin was the first one to step out.

38. **ONCE INSIDE THE ATMOSPHERE** two rotorcrafts launched from the Onyx Tower.

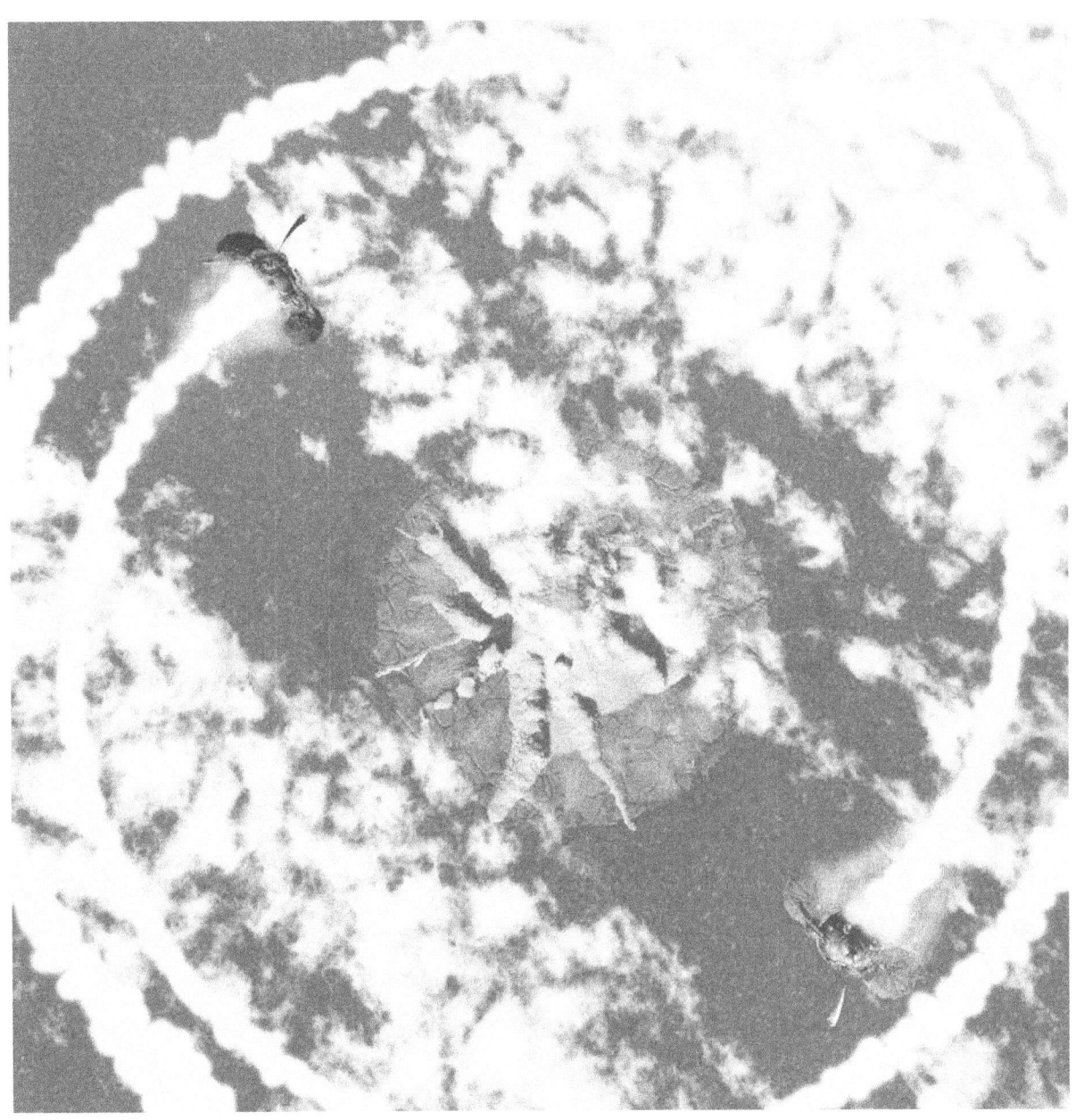

39. **AS THEY APPROACHED THE ISLAND** from above, the two rotorcrafts were now flying around each other, forming a double helix vaper trail as they descended.

Peterson got down on one knee to get a closer look at the animal tracks that were all around. "Whatever was here was big, and there was a lot of them," he said getting back to his feet.

"Yes, they look as though most all of them came out of the marsh and went back and forth from that- whatever that is over there," Burkeman said, pointing towards the dome building.

"I think I'll carry one of these until we find out what left these tracks," Peterson said as he pulled a lightning gun out of his rotorcraft.

"Peterson, I want you to keep an eye on the Rotorcraft. Everyone else, grab your gear and come with me. I want to find out what is inside that dome over there," Burkeman said.

After everyone left, Peterson got down on one knee and looked out at the marsh. Since there were no obstructions on sandy beach, he felt if anything approached, he would have plenty of time to react.

Thousands of miles away, the sky became dark as the cloud of unknown material passed over the coast of the south pole. The semi-transparent cloud cast a faint shadow across the polar ice landscape, as it passed overhead. Once directly over the south pole, it swirled into a disk, then unwound itself and slowly began its long journey back to the north pole. The probe sent from the Onyx Tower came into the atmosphere like a bright meteor, but instead of disintegrating, it slowed and altered course as it closed in on the dark cloud from behind. Moments later it entered the tail of the cloud. The probe's small collector had no problem getting samples as all the nearby, tiny black globules seemed attracted to it. It was almost as though there was some sort of magnetic reaction. After the probe had collected enough samples, it flew back up out of the atmosphere and into space. As it did, it was followed by thousands of globules, then after a moment, they all returned to the cloud. In less than an hour the probe was back on board the tower. After the probe was collected, Lionheart gave the order to move the tower back over the first point if interest, on the opposite side of the planet in the northern hemisphere.

40. HIGH IN THE UPPER ATMOSPHERE over the south pole, the tower's probe collects globule samples from the black cloud.

41. TIGHTLY SEALED IN A CLEAR CASE, the dark, featureless globules gently floated in and around each other. As Connors, Lionheart and the others observed, they maintained a constant floating motion as though they were in absolute zero gravity.

It wasn't long until the samples collected by the probe were back in the ship's science lab. Everyone wondered if the samples would give any clues as to what happened on Planet 4B and the dark moon. Tightly sealed in a clear case, the dark, featureless globules all gently floated in and around each other. As Connors, Lionheart and the others observed, the globules maintained a constant floating motion as though they were in absolute zero gravity. Whenever someone came close, the globules would float over to that side of the case. After the crewmen would back away, they would float normally again. Connors became curious as to what the possible cause of attraction could be. It wasn't long until everyone's initial interest in the samples wore off and they returned to their duties. Dr. Connors was once again alone in her lab, continuing her observation.

On Star island, Burkeman's party reached the entrance to what everyone now called Dome Mountain. The deep sandy beach had made the trek much longer than previously thought. The opening entrance was large, approximately 200 feet [61 m] wide and 250 feet [76 m] high.

"It looks like we could have just flown in here," Mullin said.

"I prefer the quiet approach," Burkeman said.

The dome's cavernous interior was somewhat visible. This was due to the other three openings that were as large as the one they entered. The center of the cavern was dark, and something was piled in it. Burkeman and the others could only see it's silhouetted form against the light from another grand opening. As they got closer, it began to look like a pile of large round rocks. The base pile was at least 150 feet [46 m] across and 90 feet [27 m] high. A cold chill came over Burkeman's party when they reached the base of the pile and discovered what it really was; massive eggs, hundreds of them. They ranged in size anywhere from one to two feet [0.3 to 0.6 m] long. Mullin swung his rifle around as if something were approaching from behind, but there was nothing there. A nest of large eggs was a dangerous place to be. He held his stance. Burkeman cautioned everyone not to disturb the eggs as they examine them. As long as the mountain's interior remained tranquil, the team felt it was safe to make their observations, that is, all except Mullin. His gun's safety was off and fully charged, ready to deliver fifty thousand volts at any threat.

42. BURKEMAN'S LANDING PARTY discovered a nest of large eggs in the center of the dome mountain's interior.

Burkeman's party became separated as each of them carried out their own examination. Unknown to anyone, Dr. Dorian took one of the smaller eggs and placed it in her backpack. When everyone was ready, Burkeman's party continued on through the far entrance to explore further.

Up in space, the onyx Tower stopped over the site where the opening to the vast underground cave network had been detected. Lionheart gave the order to make a slow descent down to forty thousand feet [12,192 m] and hold position. Two rotorcraft were dispatched to explore the area in greater detail. As they flew in low over the area, Lionheart and the others watched the live images sent back from their cameras. When he was satisfied, he gave the order to land.

The untouched glacier valley seemed endless. The surrounding, snow-covered mountains ran all the way to the distant horizon. The valley floor was filled with the sounds of animals going about their daily business amidst the constant sounds of gentle winds blowing through the tall trees. The cloudy skies started to break up as rays from the late afternoon sun began to shine through. Suddenly, the animals became silent as their world was interrupted by a low pulsing sound that came from above. A dark shadow formed in the clouds. An alien ship from another solar system was about to land. Moments later, the Onyx Tower came out of the clouds and landed in an open clearing just beyond the forest break line. The pulsing sounds stopped. After a moment, the forest was once again filled with the sounds of its inhabitants. The spars of the Onyx Tower could be seen over the treetops as it came to rest near the base of a snow-covered mountain.

"The tower is secure. We have landed Captain," Quinn said.

"We are just over two miles from the cavern's entrance. Pardon me for saying so, but you look distracted Captain," West said.

43. **THE CLOUDY SKIES STARTED TO BREAK UP** as rays from the late afternoon sun began to shine through. Suddenly, the animals became silent as their world was interrupted by a low pulsing sound coming from above. A dark shadow formed in the clouds. An alien ship from another solar system was about to land.

"I was just wondering about the dark cloud we collected samples from. I wish I knew more about it. How long will it be until it makes its way back into the northern hemisphere and reaches our position?" Lionheart asked.

"At its current rate, 23 hours and 16 minutes. It will also reach Burkeman's landing party, to the north of us, in 24 hours 37 minutes", West said.

"I can't tell you why, but I want everyone back up in space before the cloud arrives. There will be four landing parties. The maximum length of each will be five hours. We'll split the first landing party into two groups. The first group will be for support and will remain just outside the cavern entrance and maintain contact with the tower. The second group will be the science team that goes on ahead to explore. I will lead the first science team. West, Holsten, Alliot, McDoogen and Moss will come with me. Larson will lead the support team and take Dr. Kipple in case there is a medical problem and Elston for security," Lionheart said.

As they left the tower, Lionheart was reminded of the glacier valleys of western Canada. When they reached the outer entrance, they were somewhat overwhelmed by its size. The rocky, steep mountainside consisted of deep vertical furrows, suggesting that it was once under an ice flow for thousands of years. The natural entrance looked to be close to a hundred feet wide and at least two hundred feet high, giving it a gothic appearance. Approximately every hundred feet, the ridges that formed the entrance's outer boundary was repeated on a smaller scale. It gave it the appearance of a grand amphitheater. In spite of its repeated geometry, up close it looked as though it was a rare, natural formation of nature. The landing parties stopped. Lionheart ordered the ship's head geologist, Dr. Bascom, to be on the next party. After updating Thornton on their progress, Lionheart gave to order for his group to move on.

Dr. Connors continued her experiments in the science lab. Aside from their attraction to anyone coming close to their enclosure, the globules showed no reaction to any test. Connors had everything set for the next experiment. It was to test for a reaction to an intense beam of sonic energy. Working with her technicians, the sonic gun was carefully positioned near the enclosure. As the cables were connected to it, a focusing cone came loose from the barrel and fell on the floor near the base of the enclosure. Connors assistant, science technician, Stphanie Jones, leaned forward to pick it up. As her head passed near the enclosure, the floating globules slammed against the glass.

44. AS SCIENCE TECHNICIAN JONES LEANED FORWARD, the globules became violent, reacting like a dangerous animal, trying to break out of its cage.

The globules reaction was so violent, both Connors and Jones were startled. Without picking up the cone, Jones suddenly lurched backward, as though frightened by a dangerous animal. The globules began to beat hard against the enclosure as though they were trying to get at Jones. For a brief moment, Connors stood motionless with her mouth open, then motioned for Jones to step out of the room. Not wasting any time, she followed Jones out and sealed and locked the lab door behind her. Sealing the door automatically activated the bio-hazard alarm. The lab was now in full lock-down.

Looking through the thick glass window into the lab, Connors and Jones continued to watch the activity. The dark globules kept beating violently against the enclosure wall, so much so that the enclosure itself began to rock back and forth. Moments later, Thornton came to see what was happening. Having collected herself, Connors began monitoring the lab's sensors that were gathering data on all wavelengths. "Something triggered the sudden violent reaction from the globules, but what?" she thought.

Burkeman's party had reached the far shore of Star Island. There were some in his party that wished they could have gone back to the rotorcraft and flown to their current position, but Burkeman seemed determined not to miss anything. Reaching the marsh belt, they came to one of the jetties that extended out away from the island. The marsh itself looked too dangerous to enter, but the elevated jetty seemed an easy path. Skippers began to feel like he was back in Louisiana. Every now and then he noticed the ripple on the marsh land, a constant reminder that most everything was actually floating on water. He hoped there wouldn't be the equivalent of alligators around. It had become hot and humid and the constant sound of crickets (or some unknown animal that sounded like crickets) seemed almost deafening. In spite of the animal tracks and the egg nest they had discovered earlier, there was no sign of the animals themselves. It seemed as though the island was deserted.

Making their way out across the jetty, they observed several different kinds of birds and other small animals. None of them seemed threatening. The group captured many images as they walked along. Further out, away from the island, some of the marshes groundcover began to break up, revealing the seawater beneath. Up until now, Burkeman's party had been more curious than cautious, but that all changed when they began to see what looked like shark fins in the waters all around. Some of them would rise up in the marsh growth, while others came up out in the water beyond, and followed Burkeman's party as they walked along. At one point, there was some splashing activity out on open waters, away from the jetty. Several fins could be seen in the disturbance. It looked like it could be a frenzy feeding.

As the group turned their attention to observe what was happening, Breston removed his backpack and pulled out a camera. He got down on one knee to take pictures of the event. Dr. Dorian stepped back behind the others. With all the attention on what was happening, she pulled the egg she had out of her backpack and slipped it into Breston's, being careful to remove some things from his pack to compensate for weight. The disturbance ended a few minutes later. He put his pack back on and the group continued, walking further out. It wasn't much later that an unsettling feeling came over all of them. All the animal sounds they had gotten used to had abruptly stopped. Even the birds flew off. They all stopped to listen.

The silence was interrupted by something very large coming out of the water behind them. Looking back in horror, they watched as a large yellow worm like animal came up out of the marsh, onto the jetty trail behind them. With a deep growling hiss, it started to make its way toward them. Burkeman looked out at the jetty end behind them. There was only about a hundred yards left before the jetty ended at the sea. They were trapped. "Run!" Burkeman yelled as he started to run. As the others ran, Mullin released the safety from his electric gun and waited for the creature to get a little closer. As they ran, Burkeman pulled out his handheld communicator and contacted Peterson. The loud clap of thunder frightened everyone. It caused Dr. Dorian to stumble. Breston stopped and helped her back up. They began running again. After being hit by the lightning bolt from Mullin's gun, the creature stopped and lurched up and made a deep wailing sound. It then lowered itself down and continued its charge. Mullin fired another bolt. The giant worm reacted, but not as much. At first it was only hungry. Now it was angry. Every time Mullin fired his gun, the creature seemed less and less deterred. Then the unexpected happened, the electric gun overheated and burned out.

"Oh-crap!" Mullin said as he dropped his gun and started to run.

Running as hard as he could, Burkeman could see a break in the Jetty ahead. It looked to be only four to five feet across, but if he stumbled or didn't jump hard enough, he would fall over into the water. Before Burkeman could tell the others to take off their backpacks, they all jumped across, that is, all except Breston. After barely making it to the far edge, he started to stumble back into the water filled crevice. Dorian and Skippers pulled him up. At that moment, Peterson's rotorcraft appeared over Dome Mountain and was coming toward them. Burkeman felt a sense of relief as he looked back behind him and could see that they only had about a hundred feet before the jetty ended. Would Peterson get to them in time? What about Mullin? The creature was almost upon him.

As Mullin ran, he began to feel the hot stench of the creature's breath behind him. Then it stopped. Mullin continued to run but wondered why the creature had stopped. When he looked back, he saw Peterson harassing the creature from behind. Mullin was too close to the creature for Peterson to use his electric gun. Peterson feared the bolt could jump to Mullin. He gave Mullin time to distance himself, but not much. Once again, the creature continued its pursuit. As Peterson kept trying to draw the creature's attention away from Mullin, he noticed a wave forming in the marsh heading directly towards their position. Something very big was closing in. He stopped harassing the creature and flew higher.

45. **AFTER BRING HIT BY THE LIGHTNING BOLT** from Mullin's gun, the creature lurched up and made a deep wailing sound. It then lowered itself down and continued its charge.

The creature was almost upon Mullin. He thought if he jumped off the jetty, he might have a chance. Before he could do so, his foot hit a rock, and he fell forward. Just as the creature was about to strike, a herd of what looked like large, amphibious, great white sharks came up out of the water and toppled the worm creature off the jetty. The herd seemed to have no interest in Mullin, but there was still the possibility of being trampled. He quickly got back to his feet and kept running. Burkeman ran back to get Mullin. As they both jumped across to the end of the jetty, Peterson's rotorcraft landed behind them. It wasn't long until they were all crammed inside, but because of the increase in weight, Peterson told them to leave their backpacks and equipment behind. Before Breston could remove his pack, an amphibian shark came up out of the water and grabbed him from behind. Before he could react, he was pulled back down in the water. Fearing they might be next; everyone wasted no time removing their packs and getting into the rotorcraft. There would be time to grieve later.

They lifted off, but slowly. They were overloaded, and Peterson knew they had to land as soon as it was safe to do so. To everyone's shock and surprise, Breston came up out of the water and crawled back up onto the jetty. Peterson quickly dove back down as Burkeman and Mullin pulled him in. Peterson lifted off again.

"Thank God your alive man," Burkeman said, as he attended Breston's wounds.

"I don't know what happened. It was all so fast. The creature bit into my backpack and was pulling me down. As soon as I was able to get it off, the creature was gone. You know? I think it was only interested in my pack," Breston said, as he tried to regain himself.

As they looked back, they could see the giant worm continuing to battle with the shark creatures all around it. Peterson knew they couldn't stay to observe it. The rotorcraft was overloaded, and he had to find a safe place to land.

46. **AS PETERSON KEPT TRYING** to draw the creature's attention away from Mullin, he noticed a wave forming in the marsh heading directly towards their position.

47. JUST AS THE CREATURE WAS ABOUT TO STRIKE, a herd of what looked like large, amphibious, great white sharks came up out of the water and toppled the worm creature off the jetty. The herd seemed to have no interest in Mullin.

Moving ever deeper into the cavern, Lionheart's party continued to explore. As they made their way inward, much of the grand cavern's interior was just beyond the range of the amphibian's lights. At times, everyone (except West) had the feeling they were traveling outside on a dark night with no stars. For much of the time, the only reminder that the cavern was once inhabited was the relatively flat, wide road that led further into the interior. Approximately every mile or so, they passed thru a set of arches, similar to those at the entrance. At that point, West fired a forward echo pulse from the amphibian. Moments later, from the echoes received back, she was able to translate them into a clear 3D image in her mind. When the echoes came back, everyone got quiet to hear what she had to say. "It continues much the same up ahead," was all she said. At four miles in, they started to lose communication with Larson's team. Possible interference was something West had anticipated. Before starting, she had three small transmission antennas loaded on board. They were only about six feet high when fully extended and set up on a tripod at their base. Each had a seven-inch ball on top, filled with electronics and sensors. The party backed up a short distance to where a clear signal could be received, set up one of the antennas, then continued on.

First Medical Officers Log: Our voyage elapsed time is now 104 days (Oct 6th, 1627, Earth Time) 10:00 Hours:

It has been exactly one hour since Jones accidently triggered a reaction with the globules. Undeterred by their violent reaction when Technician Jones got close to the sample case, we have continued our observation. As a safety precaution, we have placed the globule case inside two larger cases. The samples continue to react violently. Watching them reminds me of a university demo model that was created to illustrate the high energy particles found in uranium. My observations so far have only raised more questions as to what this globular material could possibly consist of. The only thing that is certain is this material primarily consists of a new element, whose properties are completely unknown. I believe this is directly related to the destruction we encountered earlier on the Dark Moon and planet 4B, but exactly how, I have yet to determine. I have no rational explanation, but deep down, this globule material has left me a feeling of foreboding, as though we have captured a piece of death itself.

So far, we have discovered that it remains an inert material if it is only the size of a molecule, like the samples collected in the ruins on planet 4B. However, if it exists with mass large enough, it releases enough energy to keep itself in motion. In fact, it is always in motion. We have discovered it is able to maintain a floating state by somehow synthesizing hydrogen inside if itself, much like a balloon. Yet its means of propulsion remains a complete mystery. No expulsion of gas has been detected. No magnetic fields have been detected either. We have observed high band signals emanating from it. At first there was only occasional, periodic bursts, but after Jones got near the enclosure, the signals have become constant. Another unknown (related to its constant motion) is its power source. My observation is still preliminary, but the tests so far seem to indicate that it draws power from its own atomic mass, yet there is no trace of harmful rays of uranium. Another aspect, as yet explained, is its ability to exist in the form of a moving cloud that flies in such a pattern and course that ensures it will pass over the entire surface of planet 4A. As it flies from pole to pole and back again, over and over, it's almost as though the cloud was looking for something.

J. Connors: First Medical Officer

Burkeman's rotorcraft landed close by the other rotorcraft at their initial landing site. Shortly after, Burkeman's party boarded both rotorcrafts and flew to a high point at the island's center where they could observe the marsh area from a safe distance. As they looked out using their telescopes, they could see that the amphibious sharks were still battling the giant yellow worm. As the minutes passed, the giant yellow worm was beginning to show signs of slowing. Eventually, it was simply too tired to defend itself. When it finally stopped moving, the sharks swarmed to one side of the worm, and moving collectively, rolled it across the marsh towards the islands interior. As they reached further inland, the sharks continued to roll and push the worm up out of the marsh and onto the beach. It was at this point Burkeman's party noticed that the sharks had elephant like tusks they used to bulldoze the worm. Everyone was also surprised at their clear display of intelligence. They rolled the worm up not far from the dome. Once there, they positioned the worm on its back with its belly directly exposed to the sun. As they did so, the worm continued to make faint movements.

"That worm won't last long now," Burkeman said.

"It's like a turtle on its back in the desert sun," Dorian said.

"I think they captured that worm to feed their young when they hatch," Breston said.

Just as Breston spoke, a shark came up out of the swamp carrying an egg in its mouth. It was hard to tell, but it also had what looked like a strap from a backpack in its mouth. Carefully looking through her telescope, Dorian could see that the strap was from Breston's backpack.

"Well, at least now we know what made all the tracks in the sand. I never imagined being in a place where sharks lay eggs, are intelligent and amphibious," Peterson said.

"Were nearly a thousand lightyears from Earth. I think this is just the tip of an iceberg," Burkeman said.

48. **LOOKING THROUGH HER TELESCOPE,** Dorian could see the amphibian was carrying an egg in its mouth and what looked like a strap from Breston's backpack.

The City

They were almost 12 miles [19.3 km] into the interior. The last transmission antenna was set up.

"I chose to use a land vehicle because I thought the cavern would get a lot smaller once we got deeper into the interior. But from the size of this cavern, we could have sent rotorcraft. West, signal Larson that we are heading back," Lionheart said.

"Captain, I would like to fire another echo pulse first," West requested.

"Go ahead," Lionheart responded.

The pulse was fired. As before, everyone got quiet. A moment later, they could see West had a puzzled look on her face. Surprised by her reaction, Lionheart became curious.

"Wait. Just a moment. Just a moment. Captain there is something up ahead, approximately one-half mile," West said.

"What is it?" Lionheart asked.

"Up ahead the road ends. There appears to be a deep chasm just beyond.

"Let's check it out," Lionheart said, as he motioned at McDoogen to drive on.

Moments later, they stopped on the edge of a chasm. Just ahead of them was a wide bridge entrance, but a short distance further the bridge was out. It was made of stone. Holston and Alliot wondered how old it might be. The entrance of the bridge was flanked by two grand obelisks. They both had markings on them. Everyone went out to get a closer look. The amphibian's lights revealed only the sharp drop off and bridge entrance ahead of them, but nothing further. There was nothing but darkness beyond. Lionheart felt he was at the edge of the world. Also, communication with Larson was breaking up. West fired another echo pulse. She had a clear 3D vision of the pulse wave in her mind. At first there was nothing. Then she saw the far bank with the opposite side of the bridge and just beyond, several buildings. After Lionheart viewed the image inside the amphibian, he decided it was safe to launch a flair.

49. **LIONHEART'S AMPHIBIAN STOPPED** at the edge of a great chasm.

"We are ready sir. I have the flare set for a ten second delay," McDoogen said.

"Very good McDoogen. Launch the Flare," Lionheart commanded.

"Aye sir"

The small rocket fired away into the darkness ahead. Lionheart looked at his pocket watch. At the stroke of ten seconds a dull point of light appeared. As the light grew brighter, the dust particles in the cavern's air became luminous, creating a transparent ball that expanded outward. Seconds later, the cavern ceiling became visible. A moment later they could see the buildings on the far bank. The site before them was almost overwhelming. Even Lionheart felt a little uneasy.

"How is it possible that a cavern this size can even exist? The far bank looks to be at least two miles away. Back on Earth a cavern this size would simply collapse under its own weight," Lionheart said quietly.

"Actually, it is just over two miles [3.2 km] to the far side. You are correct in suggesting that this cavern, under normal Earth conditions, shouldn't exist, however since entering the mountain I have detected a unique mineral pattern in the road, walls and ceiling. There are unusual veins of a diamond/granite running throughout. It is in a kind of fish net pattern, all around us. I suggest it is the reason a cavern this grand can exist, and I'm quite certain, it is not natural. Captain, I would like to return to the ship and prepare a mind drone. I believe it would be the best way to explore further. In order for it to work, we will need to bring in one, possibly two more transmission antennas to maintain clear communication with the drone after it passes beyond this point," West said.

The light from the flare began to fade, then it was dark again. After Holston and Alliot had photographed the obelisks and taken samples for carbon dating, they started back. Once clear communication was restored, Lionheart canceled the next amphibian expedition, and dispatched a rotorcraft to set up the antennas that would allow a clear signal at the cliffs edge. In Lionheart's mind, the clock was ticking. He thought about the Burkeman party, and how he would have to retrieve them long before the dark cloud was back in the northern hemisphere. He knew he only had approximately 11 hours before the clouds arrival.

50. **SECONDS LATER AS THE FLARE'S LIGHT** became brighter, the cavern ceiling became visible. A moment later they could see the buildings on the far bank. The site before them was almost overwhelming. Even Lionheart felt a little uneasy.

First Medical Officers Log: Our voyage elapsed time is now 104 days (Oct 6th, 1627, Earth Time) 13:00 Hours:

It has been exactly four hours since Jones accidently triggered a reaction with the globules. For a time, I thought we would have to take even more restrictive measures to further isolate them. However, the level of their activity has significantly decreased. We have re-entered the lab, but as a precaution, we kept the globules in a triple enclosure. Technician Jones has suggested the possibility they might be attracted to brain wave activity. As farfetched as it seems, I find myself curious about the possibility. The high band signals detected from the globules suggest the possibility there may be a form of communication between them. Jones has suggested, if they can detect high band signals, they may also be able to detect the faint electromagnetic brain waves emitted from most animals.

To test Jones theory, a small transmitter has been positioned directly next to the globules inner enclosure. At first, I plan to broadcast the brain waves of lower animals and slowly move up the intelligence level to those of higher animals. If there is any truth to her theory, the globules should react accordingly. If it does react the way she predicts it will, my next question is why.

J. Connors: First Medical Officer

Five hours after they departed, the Lionheart's exploration party returned to the tower. West recharged herself and had Petrov prepare a mind drone. Deep down, Lionheart always felt somewhat uneasy around the mind drone. Whenever it flew, Lionheart had the impression it was a like a ghostly, floating, head looking for its severed body. West constructed it for herself. It basically consisted of a mechanical head (very similar to her own) wearing a crown of four evenly spaced propellers. West seldom used the drone, but when she did, she was able to temporally transfer her mind into it, and it obeyed her every command. When asked about it, she said it would be the equivalent to a human having consciousness outside their body.

51. AS CHIEF ENGINEER PETROV PREPARES THE MINE DRONE for flight, West goes through recharging.

First Medical Officers Log: Our voyage elapsed time is now 104 days (Oct 6th, 1627, Earth Time) 15:00 Hours:

The brain wave experiments are continuing. At 14:30 hours, the brain wave transmitter was set for the average intelligence of a dog. At first the globules started to become active and floated to the side of the enclosure. It is almost as though they were curious. After several moments, their movement activity returned to normal, and they floated back to their initial position. At 15:00 hours the brain wave transmitter was set for the average intelligence of a chimpanzee. I'm about to start this phase of the experiment and wanted Captain Lionheart to attend, but he is unable. Instead, he will be monitoring the mind drone of West as she flies it deeper into the caves interior. After hearing about the discovery of a subterranean settlement, I also wanted to attend, but I feel an urgency to learn as much as we can about the globules. I can't overcome my continued feeling of anxiety. The globule cloud is due to arrive here in approximately nine hours.

J. Connors: First Medical Officer

Down in Petrov's lab, adjacent to the launch bay, West sat out in the open with a helmet on. It had several cables coming out of it that ran across the floor to a nearby console. Petrov stood behind her as he made the final adjustments to her helmet.

"That should do it. You should have complete thought control now," he said, as he took a step back. The lab's viewing screens gave everyone complete 360° views from the drone's cameras.

"Drone systems diagnostics are complete. Start motors," West thought as the drone out in the launch bay came to life. "I am ready to proceed Captain".

"Proceed West," Lionheart said.

Even though he was focused on the drone's monitors, out of the corner of his eye, Lionheart could see the drone lifting off and flying out of the launch bay. The drone flew up and away from the tower. West kept the drone above the treetops. Occasionally, they could see the path the amphibian was on earlier.

"What is that?" Petrov said, pointing at one of the monitors.

"It looks like some kind of bird," Lionheart said.

As everyone watched the monitors, a colorful bird flew around the drone, then started attacking. West continued to fly the drone ahead but was constantly dodging the bird.

"West, we don't have time for this," Lionheart quietly said, as he started to get annoyed.

"Understood Captain," West said, as the mind drone discharged a small lightning bolt at the bird.

There was a loud screech as some feathers were blown off its tail. It turned and dove back down into the forest. A short time later the drone reached the entrance. As it transitioned from daylight into darkness its lights came on. At first it was difficult to see anything. West flew the drone low until the ground path became visible. Beyond the limit of the drone's lights was darkness. Lionheart had the impression he was driving down a dark country road. The drone was flying along much faster than the amphibian.

"We should reach the edge of the cliff in no time," Lionheart quietly said to Petrov.

"At this speed, I estimate just under four minutes," West said.

After reaching the cliff, the drone flew out over the bridge entrance, then beyond into the darkness. The other side was beyond the drone's lights. The monitors became completely dark. In her mind, West could clearly see the drone's gauges. It was flying straight and level. The far cliffs came into view at the exact time she expected to see them. Everyone became silent as the drone flew over the far side of the bridge. As expected, the city was completely deserted. On all the empty streets the drone passed over, West detected large deposits of calcium in the soil. All of the buildings had the same puncture and scratch marks that were found on Planet 4B.

52. WITH HER MIND CONNECTED TO THE DRONE, West gave the command to lift off. Moments later, not far from the tower, the drone dealt with an unexpected visitor.

53. **UPON REACHING THE DESERTED CITY,** the drone scans one of the buildings to learn it's age.

"Captain?" West asked.

"Yes, I see it. What ever happened on Planet 4B also happened here," Lionheart said.

"Curious," West said.

"What is it?" Lionheart asked.

"Some of the buildings encountered here are of the same architectural design as those found in the Earth underworld," West said.

"Yes, I thought they looked familiar," Lionheart quietly said.

"I remember this underworld," Petrov said.

"Yes. The only entrance was at a remote location in what is now Eastern Turkey. The great war of 1700 was fought over who would control the only way in. How ironic that the intense fighting caused a quake that sealed the entrance forever, or at least until someone can figure out a way to reach it again," Lionheart said.

"The architectural similarities between them suggest a possible link of some kind," West said.

"West, I'm curious to know the approximate age of this city, I would like a sample for carbon dating," Lionheart said.

West flew the drone over to the nearest building and did a brief, close up scan. Afterword, the drone flew up and continued. "Telemetry from the scan has been received. We should have the results in..."

"Wait. Turn to the right. Yes. Those look like massive power conduits. Magnify," Lionheart said, interrupting West.

As everyone watched, West focused the drones forward camera on large, distant power conduits that were just visible over the roof tops. Before Lionheart could give the command to fly closer, West headed for the area of interest. As the drone got closer, there were slight interruptions in its signal. With each break in the signal, the drone wobbled slightly. West landed it on the nearest roof top, to keep it from crashing.

"West?"

"Signal interference Captain, I'm going to boost the gain, but we are reaching the limit of the drone's range. I have anticipated the possibility of this," West said, just as she gave a mental command for a second, drone to be launched from the tower. Lionheart caught it out of the corner of his eye as it flew out of the bay. One thing about West he was always impressed with, was her ability to always be several steps ahead in any situation. To him, it was like playing a game of chess with someone who could clearly see every possible move you could make and know all of the counter moves required to win the game in the shortest time possible.

Everyone took a small break as the second drone was flown into place, to act as a signal carrier for the first drone. Thirty minutes later, the second drone landed on one of the roof tops at the closest edge of the city. "Full signal has been restored, Captain," West said as the first drone lifted off the roof top. Moments later, it reached the power conduits. After arriving, West had the drone pan left. The conduits lead out to another cavern. West followed them to a burned out domed building. As the drone got closer, everyone could clearly see it was the remains of a power plant. As the drone hovered just over the edge of the plant, the silent, cold power generators became visible.

"Captain, I'm curious what this power planet was used for," Petrov said.

"What do you mean?" Lionheart asked.

"From the drone's images, it looks like this plant was capable of producing a tremendous amount of power, yet the conduits coming out of it, lead past the city," Petrov said.

"Your right. West, follow the conduits. Let's find out what all this power was used for- Wait," Lionheart said interrupting himself. "Can you see that? Something is moving just off to the right."

"Curious," West said as she maneuvered the drone to the right and dropped down into the plant. There was a dull black, bubble-like object floating just above the base of a nearby generator. As the drone got closer, they could see it was the same material Connors had in the lab. The way it constantly changed its shape gave Lionheart the impression they were looking at something underwater. After a moment, it floated closer. West slowly maneuvered the drone to keep it from drifting into the rotor blades.

"Drone sensors indicate it is the same material as the cloud sample we extracted earlier. Interesting. It behaves is such a way that would suggest it is attracted to the drone in some way," West reported.

"It would seem not all of this material is in the large cloud that is headed this way," Petrov said.

"Yes, but what is it doing here and why would it be here? West lets return to the power conduits. I want to find out where they go," Lionheart said.

"Yes Captain," West said as the drone flew up, out of the power plant and started to follow the conduits.

Looking at the rear camera screen, Lionheart and Petrov noticed, slowly from a distance, a school of dark globules was following. They moved much the same way floating debris might briefly follow the wake of a passing ship. Only in this case, it kept following. In the passing minutes, more globules appeared. West had no trouble keeping the drone out ahead of them. The conduits led to another large cavern, further beyond the city. They turned downward into a large opening. West started getting signal interference again. She re-positioned the signal drone out at the city's edge to restore it as best she could. As she did so, a few globules appeared. Turning her attention back to the first drone, she started to follow the conduits down into the vertical tunnel. The drone descended nearly a thousand feet [305m]. As the drone cameras continually panned around during descent, more dark globules appeared, but in this case, they were all clinging to the pipes and walls all around but started to float freely when the drone neared.

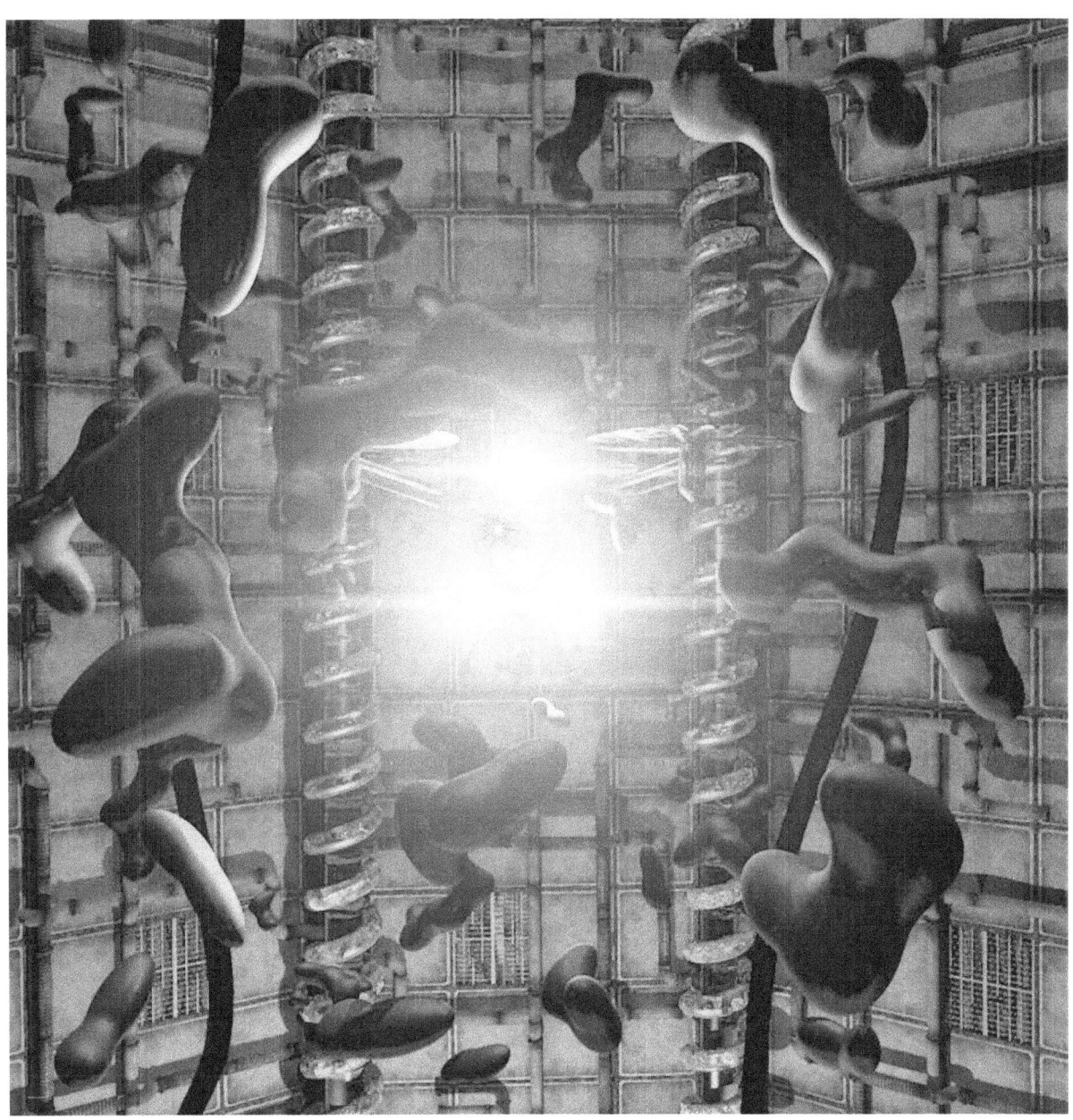

54. DEEPER IN THE SHAFT, the drone encountered active globules.

On the floor of the grand shaft, the conduits terminated into a burned-out complex of transformers and other large machinery. Several smaller conduits led into another, small chamber. Even more black globules became visible. Most of them were clinging to surfaces, but some came loose and floated up pasted the drone as it flew by.

"It that what I think it is?" Lionheart quietly said.

"It appears to be Captain," West said as she flew the drone closer.

In the center of the large domed chamber was a lower half ring. From the remains of it, both Lionheart and West could see it was the same kind as one that was built years ago back on Earth by his associate, Margret Dana. Back in the 1830's she began her experiments in the new field of inter-dimensional physics. She was interested in developing a portal doorway that would allow someone to step from England to America in an instant. She was successful, but the portal was never completely stable. In spite of that, her discovery led to the development of the internal drive engine. As Lionheart looked at the images from the drone, it was clear that whoever lived here, had also discovered portal technology.

The chamber was filled with globules of dark material. For a moment, Lionheart had the impression the material was waiting for someone to come thru the portal. As the drone passed over and around the ring, more and more globules broke away from what they were clinging to and began floating around. At this point, West continued to fly the drone to keep its propellers from hitting them. This was complicated by signal interference again.

"Captain, there seems to be an inscription of some kind near the bottom. Signal interference is making this difficult," West said, as the drone hovered near the portal ring.

"The drone is well within signal range. She shouldn't be getting any interference," Petrov quietly said to Lionheart.

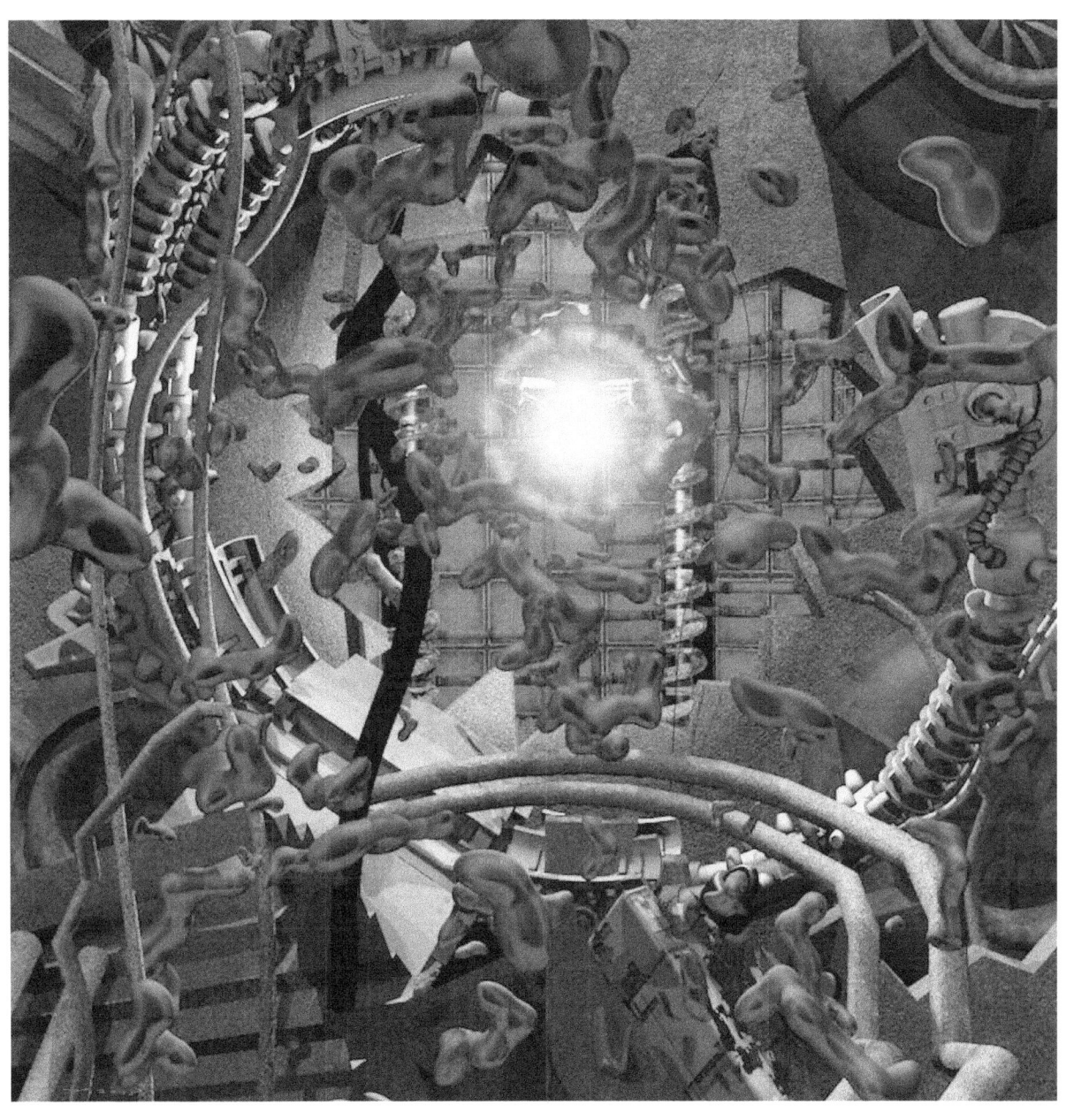

55. THE DRONE DISCOVERES what looks like the remains of portal technology.

"The interference is coming from the globules. They're emitting a very faint ultra-high frequency signal between them. I'm going down to have a closer look. Some of them are blocking the inscription. I'll try to remove them with the drone's arm. Because of the signal interference, I will have to split-mind the drone. This means we can watch, but because the drone will start operating using its own mind, we will no longer have any direct control over it. This will take a minute," West said.

"Proceed West," Lionheart said.

Up in the science lab, Dr. Connors continued with her experiments.

First Medical Officers Log: Our voyage elapsed time is now 104 days (Oct 6th, 1627, Earth Time) 17:00 Hours:

At 15:30 hours we transmitted the same brainwaves that would be emitted by a chimpanzee. In an instant, the globules became violent, once again bouncing off the walls of the inner enclosure. Also, at the same time, they emitted an ultra-high frequency. I immediately cut off the brainwave signal. The violent activity continued for just under seven minutes, then diminished back to its normal state. However, during the violent period, all but one of the glass enclosure panels were badly damaged, making it almost impossible to observe them. I have decided to postpone the tests until the globules can be transferred to another enclosure.

J. Connors: First Medical Officer

"Captain Lionheart? Thornton here."

"Lionheart here. Go ahead Thornton."

"Captain. Our probes circling the planet indicate the dark cloud has changed its heading. It has entered the upper hemisphere and is now heading directly for us. ETA is 57 minutes," Thornton said.

"All right Thornton, prepare to lift off. Mr. Petrov, power up the ship. I'm going to wait just long enough for West's drone to read the inscription, then we are getting out of here," Lionheart commanded.

"I'm turning on the drone's mind now, Captain," West said.

As they watched, West gave up control of the drone. It was now under the control of its own electronic mental system. It was now independent, thinking for itself. It is as though a temporary replica of West's mind was copied and loaded into the drone directly. As they watched, the drone's mechanical arm began removing globules to see the inscription. As it did so, more of them began floating nearby.

"The drone is now independent," West said as she reached up and removed her headset. Almost at once the globules nearby attached themselves to the drone's arm. After doing so, they changed their form into what looked like headless, black spiders. Almost at once there came a high-pitched sound as the dark material became active. The sound came through the audio in the launch bay. Lionheart and the others covered their ears. In response, West cut the drone's audio signal. The drone lunged backward as it tried to shake the spiders off, but it was to no avail, as they hung on tightly, using their legs to get a tight grip. Not wasting any time, the drone flew out of the chamber with hundreds of black floating globules in close pursuit.

At that very moment in the science lab, the globules were being transferred via means of a transparent tube. Suddenly, without warning, parts of them began to form into sharp spikes. They once again became violent and began hitting the walls of the transfer tube. They used their spikes to penetrate the glass. Connors ordered everyone out of the lab. Seconds later, the tube shattered. The bio alarm sounded as the lab doors began to close. A technician who was standing near the tube, slipped on broken glass and fell as he tried to get out. Before he could react, the globules were upon him. The doors to the lab closed and sealed. Looking back through the door windows, Connors and Jones watched in horror as the globules on the technician changed form into what looked like some kind of spider-like animal. Within seconds, the walls of the lab turned red as he was completely shredded. They tore into him like a hoard of flying piranha. Even his bones were broken up into fine rubble. After he was gone, they began hitting against the walls of the lab again. Connors lunged back as several globules smashed against the lab door window.

56. **AFTER THE DRONE BECAME INDEPENDENT,** the globules attacked.

57. **CONNERS LUNGED BACK** as the globules smashed against the lab door.

Down in the launch bay, Lionheart paid little attention to the lab alarm, as he continued to watch the drone try to fly away from the black globules. The spiders on the drone's arm began to make their way up to the drone's head. The drone's lightning defense weapon had no effect on the attacking globules. As they reached the drone face, small spearheads formed out of their back legs allowing them to puncture and lock on. They relentlessly kept jabbing into the drone. Little puffs of smoke come from the drone as its electronics started to short out. The drone flew up out of the shaft like a wounded bird, weaving back and forth. In a great swarm, the globules followed. One by one the viewing screens went out as the spiders punched out the drone's cameras. It just reached the edge of the city as the forward camera showed the stomach of a spider, then it was gone.

"West, switch to the transmitter drone," Lionheart commanded.

The view from the transmitter drone came on, just in time to see the initial drone consumed by the globules. In seconds, it was shredded completely. As everyone watched, small bits and pieces of it sparkled in the lights of the second drone as they rained down on the roof tops. The globules swirled around then started for the second drone. West turned the drone around and began to fly across the chasm, away from the city. Just as the other side of the chasm came onto view, the second drone was overwhelmed by the globules and transmission was lost. Seconds later, the nearby transmitter stopped. After a brief moment, the next closest one stopped transmitting.

Captain, the transmission antennas are going out, one by one. The globules are following the signal back to us," West reported.

"Mr. Thornton. Get us out of here. Get the tower back into space now!" Lionheart commanded.

An alarm sounded throughout the ship, warning the crew to brace themselves for increased gravity as the ship started to lift off. Everyone felt a strong vibration as the tower came alive. Lionheart and West made their way to the bridge. As the tower rose up into the clouds, the large black swarm of globules came out of the cavern entrance. The bird that had encountered West's drone earlier, unknowingly flew in the path of the swarm. In less than a second nothing but blood, bones and feathers rained down on the forest below. Moving in a spiral, the swarm began to follow behind the ascending tower. But after it reached the upper atmosphere, it stopped and began swirling around, forming what looked like a miniature hurricane.

Joined by two, armed security guards, Connors watched as the globules in the lab continued to smash against the lab windows.

"Sooner or later, they are going to get out. We have to seal off this corridor," Connors said as they backed away slowly. At that moment, they broke through the lab window. With the security guards right behind her, Connors ran to the doors at the far end of the corridor. As they reached the door, one of them stopped, turned and fired his electric rifle at the globules. The lightning energy blew some of the globules apart but didn't stop all of them. The other security guard pushed Connors through the doorway and closed it behind her. He turned and began firing his gun. Connors looked on through the door's windows. The guards continued firing on the globules. They were blown apart with each blast from the lightning guns. But seconds later, they would regather and continue their attack. Each time, they would get a little closer to the guards. One of the guns lost its charge. Unable to hold them off, the globules swarmed around the guards and within seconds, they were gone. Only blood and small fragments of flesh and bone remained. Horrified, Connors continued to run as the globules began bouncing all around the sealed corridor. Before turning away from the door windows, she noticed there were more of them. "But where did they come from?" she wondered.

"We are in space now," Thornton reported.

"Are they following?" Lionheart asked.

58. **AFTER PUSHING DR. CONNERS OUT** and sealing the door behind her, the two security guards tried to stop the globules after they broke out of the lab.

"Negative. They appear to be forming in a circular cloud pattern in the upper atmosphere below us," West responded.

"Captain!" Thornton said alarmingly.

"Yes! I know! The bio alarms! West, do you have anything on the situation?" Lionheart asked.

"Ship indicates the bio lab has been compromised. I'm putting the recorded images up now, Captain. All corridors leading to that lab have been sealed off. Three crew are dead," West reported, as everyone watched the carnage.

"My God," Lionheart said quietly.

"Captain, this is Connors. I'm in corridor C7 near the bio lab. The globules were contained in the corridor, but they are getting out into the air vents. They kill everyone they come in contact with," Connors sounded hysterical.

"Damn. West, where could they have gone?" Thornton asked.

"Just a moment," West said as she pulled the ships ducting plans into her mind. "There are three possibilities."

"Captain. I just got a report from observation room 11F. When our men got there, everyone there was dead," Moss reported.

"How many?" Lionheart asked.

"There is no way to tell. The room is saturated with blood, flesh and bone. Captain, they were completely shredded. Sir, a report came in of another attack on F deck. I have to go." Moss said as he left the bridge.

"Captain, there is no way to stop what is happening by conventional means. If this continues at the current rate, all living crew will be terminated in three hours and fifty-three minutes. I have an idea and would like to proceed," West said.

"Very well, we know electric guns can't stop them," Lionheart said as he remembered the security guards being killed outside of the bio lab.

"Thank you, Captain. You will be revived when it is over," West said.

"What?" Lionheart asked. Just at that moment there was a popping sound, and the air pressure suddenly dropped all over the ship. Everyone fell to the floor unconscious. West had already commanded several mechanical crew to place explosives in dome three along with a transmitter. As soon as it was in place, the transmitter began sending out strong brainwave signals, equivalent to a population of ten thousand people. As West expected, all globules began heading for dome three. Once they entered that chamber, West ordered the mechanical crew to seal it off. She then detonated the explosives. In an instant, the dome and everything in it was blown out into space. All globule material was off the ship. West then commanded the ship to raise the air pressure and restore oxygen levels. She then kneeled and helped Lionheart sit up as he regained consciousness.

"West, did you have to knock me out?" Lionheart asked, as he tried to regain himself.

"It was necessary. There was no time to explain my plan. All of the globules are off the ship, but they are not destroyed. They are now circling the ship from an approximate distance of ten miles. In the atmosphere below us, the globule cloud has arrived and appears to be merging with the mass we discovered," West said.

"I have a horrible headache. Help me get to me feet," Lionheart said, as West helped him stand up.

"Thanks," Lionheart said.

Everyone on the bridge was regaining their senses.

59. WEST EXPLODES DOME THREE.

60. **THE ENTIRE GLOBULE MASS** on the planet began to converge in the upper atmosphere.

"I have posted mechanical crew throughout the ship at all critical positions until the crew is fully revived. Captain, the two globule clouds on the planet below have joined and are now gaining strength. Wait…," she said interrupting herself. 'The globule cloud is now a massive single entity, and it is now heading into space. It's coming here," she reported.

"Mr. Quinn, get us further out into space, at least one hundred thousand miles," Lionheart commanded.

"Aye sir," Quinn responded.

Everyone felt a heavy sensation as the tower began to move further out into space. The globules held their circular orbit at first, then began to form in a helix pattern as they followed the tower.

"Mr. Petrov," Lionheart called out.

"Petrov here, Captain," Petrov said in a somewhat groggy voice.

"Bring the shields to full power."

"Aye sir, bringing the shields to full power. Shields are powering up now," Petrov reported.

As the Onyx Tower's shields powered up, a transparent bubble field began to form around the ship. As the globules caught up to the ship, most were incinerated when they made contact with the shield. Sensing danger, the remaining globules continued to circle the ship, staying just outside the shield.

"So, this is what attacked the alien ship we encountered on the rogue moon. But why? It just doesn't make any sense," Lionheart said.

"Based on my observations, I have a plausible theory, Captain," West said.

"I would like to hear it," Connors said as she entered the bridge.

"I believe it is an automated support system for colonization, that was developed by a highly advanced race," West said.

"How can something that monstrous be considered a support system?" Connors asked.

"I was not attempting to access what we would consider its moral nature, Doctor. It seems to have been launched from an unknown origin, perhaps many light years away. From your lab tests, it seems to only react violently to any intelligent form of life. The trigger is our faint electro-magnetic brain waves. It's sensing ability is so acute that it can distinguish between intelligent and non-intelligent life forms. By first terminating any intelligent life, it effectively removes that obstacle, thereby making the process of invasion and conquest much more efficient for its creators," West said.

"So, this system firsts eliminates any opposition the invaders might encounter. What comes after that? What is its second objective?" Thornton asked.

"I believe it is...," West stopped herself. "Wait. Captain, ship's sensors indicate a second globule cloud will arrive here in under 14 minutes.

Everyone turned their attention to the bridge viewing screens. The camera below revealed a swirling dark, semi-transparent, hurricane mass heading up straight towards them. As it approached, everyone braced for impact.

"My God," Quinn said, quietly to himself.

At first it slammed into the ship's intense electro-magnetic shields. Much of it burned up as it did so. The few globules that actually got close to the tower were blown apart by a lightning discharge. Even though blown apart, the misty remains eventually merged back together, and came at the tower once more. It was then, everyone knew the globules had a way of somehow renewing themselves. Lionheart knew the ships power couldn't be maintained forever. When the larger globule cloud from below encountered the shield only a small percentage of it came through. Most of it moved out and merged with the other globules that came from the caverns on the planet below. The globule cloud had now formed into a large ring that was circling the tower. Because of their dark color, they could only be seen when they passed in front of planet 4A.

61. THE ONYX TOWER COMES UNDER ATTACK.

For the next several hours, portions of the globule cloud ring would break off to attack the tower. It was almost as though the cloud had a collective intelligence and was testing the shield for weakness. After a series of attacks, much of the cloud had diminished. Many globules had burned up in the tower's shields. There was a standoff. Lionheart and Petrov knew when it was over, it was likely the tower would not have the power to sustain itself, and most likely, would tumble back into the atmosphere to a fiery end. Still, if they did nothing the cloud would kill everyone off in time. At least Burkeman and his party would be safe, at least for a while. The attacks stopped. Petrov reported the power was down by 73%. Lionheart believed the tower's remaining power would be enough to destroy what remained of the cloud.

Lionheart didn't know whether or not to be relieved or concerned when the globule cloud broke away from circling the tower and formed into spinning disk. At the very center of it the globules began clumping together. The center form was constantly changing shape as the smaller globules began pouring into it. The cloud began to resemble a small, black asteroid with thousands and thousands of small globules all around it. As the tower and cloud passed over to the dark side of the planet, West switched the bridge screens to see infrared. The dark globule material appeared bright yellow/orange. During the battle, West continued to observe the globules with dispassionate curiosity. The bright infrared signature confirmed what she already knew. The globule material had an internal source of high energy, though the source of that energy was still a mystery. West recorded all the different shapes the globules became during the attacks. Now there was a standoff. Now it was morphing into something new.

Lionheart wondered what was going to happen next. When they passed over the terminator from the planet's dark side, the newly formed globule mass became clearly visible.

"Christ-all-mighty," Lionheart quietly said to himself.

The object in the center had morphed into what looked like an alien bird. Most of the globule disk was gone.

62. **AS THEY PASSED FROM THE DARK SIDE** of the planet, the globules had formed into what looked like an alien bird.

The alien bird came out of the cloud toward the tower. As it turned, a bright spot on the leading edge of each wing appeared. Seconds later they fired a large, bright energy pulse toward the tower. The tower's shields did little to stop it. With thunderous explosions, the energy pulse struck the tower, causing it to rock violently. Lionheart had designed the tower to withstand a direct hit from a uranium bomb, but he knew his ship could only stand up for so long against this kind of power. With each pass, the alien bird unleased its devastating strikes against the tower, but Lionheart struck back at the attacker with intense lightning. As it did so, pieces of the bird were blown off, but not long after, those pieces would regather with the bird. He was fighting a losing battle, and he knew it.

"We simply don't have the energy necessary to burn up the remaining globular mass, Captain," West said.

"We are not going to make it, but at least there might be a way to destroy all of it. At least Burkeman's party will survive," Lionheart said as he looked out at the alien bird turning to make another pass. Just beyond the scene of battle, was the intense solar beam coming out of the moon's inner pole.

For a moment, the bridge was quiet. Everyone knew there was a strong possibility they would not survive. West thought he was intending to lead the alien bird and the remaining globules into the moon's beam where all would be incinerated.

"I understand Captain, but how do you intend to lure that bird and globules into the beam?" West asked.

"I'm not. I'm going to blow it's remains into the beam. From the first moment we came under attack, the one consistency is the globules course. It keeps circling us over and over. If we can get close enough, we can blow it into the beam," Lionheart said.

"Captain, to do that, you would have to..." Thornton stopped himself then nodded his head.

"Mister Quinn, get us closer to moon's inner pole," Lionheart commanded.

"Aye sir," Quinn responded.

The tower started moving closer to the moon, at the same time the alien bird did little to change course and continued its attack.

"Mrs. Stone, open a channel to Burkeman's party," Lionheart commanded.

"Captain, there is a chance our shields may break up the signal," Stone responded.

"Stone, record this message".

"Recorder on, Captain", Stone responded.

"Burkeman, this is Lionheart. By the time you get this the tower will have been destroyed. For the last hour, we have been engaged against an alien entity, the same entity that consumed the inhabitants of planet 4B. We can't hold off the attack. We won't be coming back, but if all goes well, we will take the entity down with us. May God watch over you in this new world," Lionheart out.

West looked away from the bridge screen. She became quiet and distant.

"Mrs. Stone, send the message the moment our shields are down," Lionheart said. He noticed West looked disengaged.

"West, what is it? Are you alright?" Lionheart asked.

Not responding to Lionheart, she looked back at the bridge screen. The alien ship was turning to make another attack.

"Captain, our shields are coming down! Our shields are coming down! The controls are not responding! I've been locked out!" Quinn yelled.

Lionheart knew West was the only one who could lock out the controls of the tower so quickly. "West, what the hell are you doing?"

63. **LIONHEART KNEW THE TOWER** was almost out of power. In a final effort to destroy the globule alien bird, he planned to lure it into the moon's energy beam even though it meant the destruction of the tower.

The wings of the alien bird began to glow as it came closer.

"Transmission is better with the shields down, Captain," West said as she looked back at the screen. With a nod, a signal was broadcast from the tower.

"Captain, were broadcasting a signal," Stone said, as she stopped herself to listen closer. "Captain, it is the exact same signal we encountered on the dark moon."

The glow in the alien bird's wings went dark. Seconds later, the bird itself began to break up into small globules.

"That won't be necessary," West said just as Quinn was about to fire on the globule cloud. Lionheart nodded at Quinn, not to fire. The cloud passed by the tower then turned down to the planet.

"West?" Lionheart asked.

"My analysis of the alien signal from earlier is now complete, Captain. We are safe for now," West said.

"They broke off the attack. Why? What just happened?" Thornton asked.

"As I said earlier, the globules are an automated support system for colonization. It's first phase is to remove all intelligent life it encounters. Upon receiving a signal, the globule material reconfigures itself," West said.

"Reconfigures itself? What the hell for?" Thornton asked.

"Based on what we observed on the dark moon, I would say it's second phase is to become a food source for its creators," West said.

"A food source?" Dr. Connors asked

"Yes doctor, right now the remaining globule matter is headed down to an area on the planet's surface. Once there, I believe it will morph into a forest like the one we encountered," West said.

"But West, I ran tests on samples what we collected from that forest. Lab results indicated that it was a kind of petroleum-based material," Connors said.

"Precisely Doctor, this suggests that the physicality of this highly advanced race consists mostly of petroleum," West said.

"A petroleum-based life form," Lionheart said, quietly to himself.

"But West, what about planet 4B and the dark moon? Whoever was there got completely wiped out," Thornton said.

"Yes commander, the inhabitants of planet 4B did not discover the signal that turned the globules off. However, on the dark moon, they did, but not until it was too late.

"What do you mean?" Lionheart asked.

"The spherical ship we encountered on the dark moon was also of a highly advanced race. I suspect they had an electronic entity on board that was similar to me. When they encountered the globules, they instructed it to analyze and find a solution. It discovered the deactivation signal, but not before the globules had killed off the entire crew. Still operating autonomously long after the crew was gone, it continued to transmit the signal. When the globule matter morphed into a forest, no one was around to see it. After many centuries, we came upon the scene. The alien ship we encountered on the dark moon was still transmitting the signal, even after many centuries.

"Mr. Quinn, take us back to planet 4A. We need to pick up Burkeman's party," Lionheart said.

Captains Log: Our voyage elapsed time is now 106 days (Oct 8th, 1627, Earth Time)

09:00 Hours:

We managed to survive the globule battle, but it was not without losses. Twelve of my crew are dead. It all happened so fast that they scarcely knew the horror that came upon them. The remaining globule matter returned to the edge of a vast desert on the planet, just as West said it would. Once there, it morphed into a forest of black oil-based trees. West mentioned the possibility the globules also had a phase three, but she wouldn't say what it was until she had completed further analysis. I hope we never encounter the globule creators. Their open indifferent hostility to any intelligent life and the fact that their able to control matter on a molecular level, would suggest their morals are as dark as their oil-based bodies. Still, I wonder what they would think if they came to the Earth and saw us using petroleum for a lubrication and energy source.

We picked up Burkeman and the rest of his party. At first, he was angry at us for not coming back sooner, but when he learned of the globules, he was glad. As expected, planet 4A has some dangerous life forms, but no more than one would have encountered on the Earth at one time. After retrieving Burkeman's party, we landed near the newly formed black forest. Although some of the crew now refer to it as the Obsidian Forest.

With the globules no longer a threat, we have returned to the underground caverns for further exploration. West has surmised, when the globules first came to the double planet 4 system, they attacked 4B first. When its devastation was spreading out of control, the inhabitants on 4A took whatever precautions they could and tried to fortify themselves. Based on what we have discovered so far that fortification failed. Since our first visit to the underground city, more evidence has been uncovered, suggesting a possible direct link with the underworld on Earth. The first aspect was the architecture which West observed. As more and more rotorcraft missions were flown into the city, clues have turned up that re-confirm the inhabitants here may very well have been human. The strongest clue was the discovery of a park filled with statues. At first, the area was thought to be only a reservoir of shattered marble. However, when expedition teams began sifting through the rubble, several pieces were discovered that had unmistakable human form. It was very similar to what we discovered on 4B. The pinnacle of this discovery was a partially broken face of a beautiful woman. The crew already refers to it as the Lady of Pangaea. I plan to remain here for a time to allow for a thorough exploration of the caverns and repair the ship.

P. M. Lionheart: Captain

Not long after the Onyx Tower returned to the site to explore the underground city, most all the crew had time to explore this newfound world. There were only two rules; Always carry a weapon and never be alone. It wasn't long until hanson units armed with lighting guns were stationed all around the tower. The crew learned of some of the local predators after they started to set up repair camps. It was late afternoon.

The rule of being alone was ignored by crewman Ivanov. The quiet area he stood in was exactly as his Guardian described. Looking down at his time piece, Ivanov saw he was on time. As instructed, he removed a small metallic sphere from his pocket and placed it on the ground in front of him and stepped away. At that moment the object began to crackle and glow with blue lightning. The light coming from it was so bright, Ivanov had to turn away. A doorway of light was opening. When the light and sound faded away, Ivanov slowly turned back but kept his head down. The Guardian stood before him.

"Everything happened exactly as you said it would," Ivanov said.

"Did you collect the specimens I asked for?"

"Yes. I was able to retrieve them just after the globules destroyed the medical lab. During all the chaos, no one saw me. May I ask what they are for?" Ivanov said as he handed them up to the Guardian. He was careful not to look up at the Guardian's face.

"They will become historic legends. You must return to the tower. Soon after you have seen the Eye of Crystor, you will see me again," the Guardian said in a deep voice as he concealed the bottled samples in his clock.

"But, Master, what is the Eye of Crystor?" Before Ivanov could look up there was another blinding blue light and suddenly, the Guardian was gone.

64. SOON AFTER REPAIR WORK began the crew realized the ruins of the nearby underground city provided a grand source of various materials that could easily be refabricated. At the suggestion of several crew members, it was decided that dome three would be rebuilt as a transparent dome with a park like setting in the interior. Captain Lionheart agreed. He felt it would be good for morale.

65. SEVERAL MISSIONS WERE FLOWN to the newly formed Obsidian Forest in a desert valley not far from the tower's landing site.

66. LIONHEART MET WITH JANE McRANDEL, the ships head cartographer, to document the planets and moons encountered after leaving Earth. Even though McRandel said the maps after leaving Alpha Centauri would be vague and preliminary at best, Lionheart insisted. He said to name Planet 4A "Pangaea", the hollow moon orbiting Pangaea "Crystor", and planet 4B "Torlon". When asked why, he took a deep breath and said in a voice he heard in a dream and told him to do so.

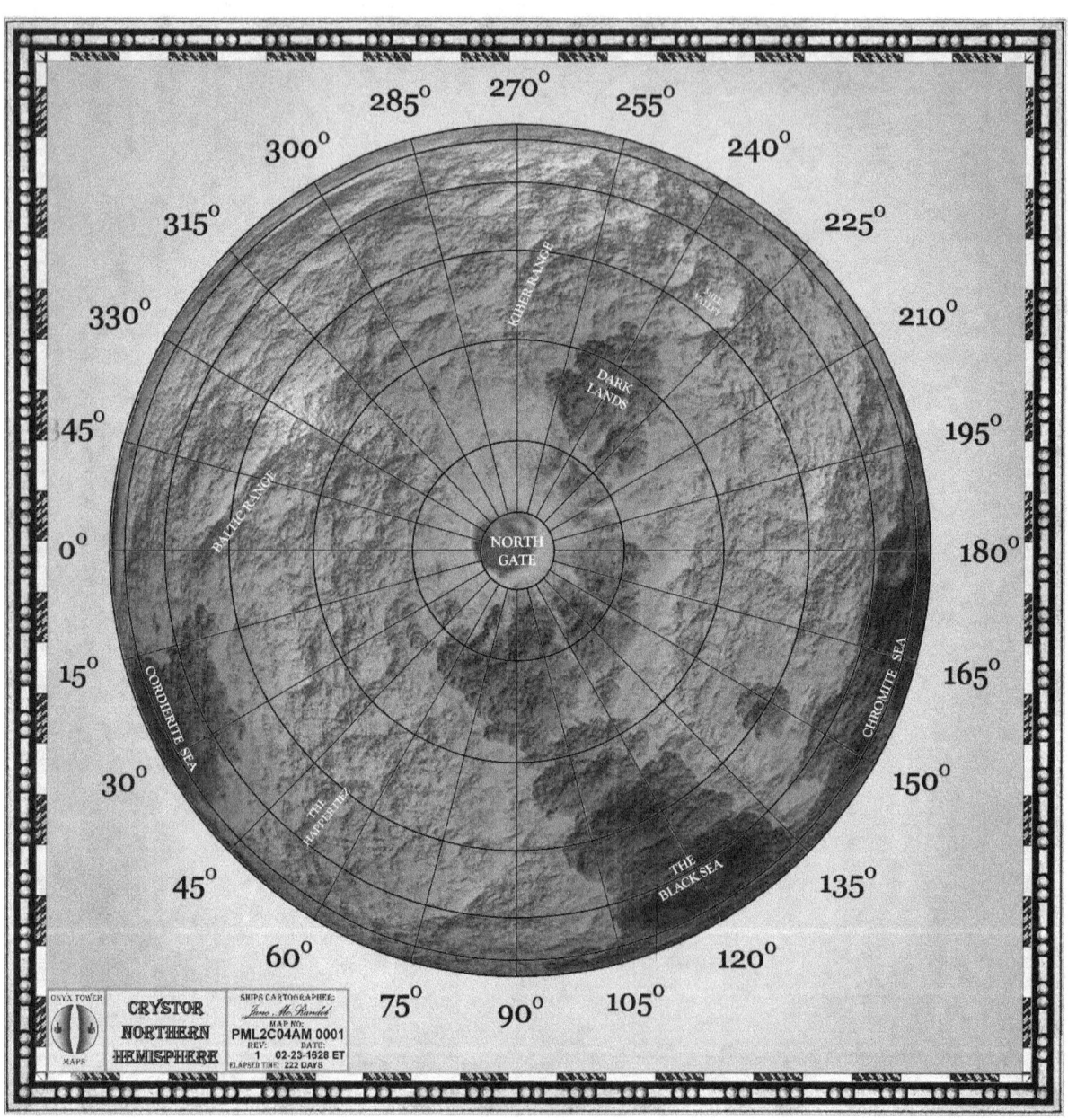

67. CRYSTOR NORTHERN HEMISPHERE that faces out into space.

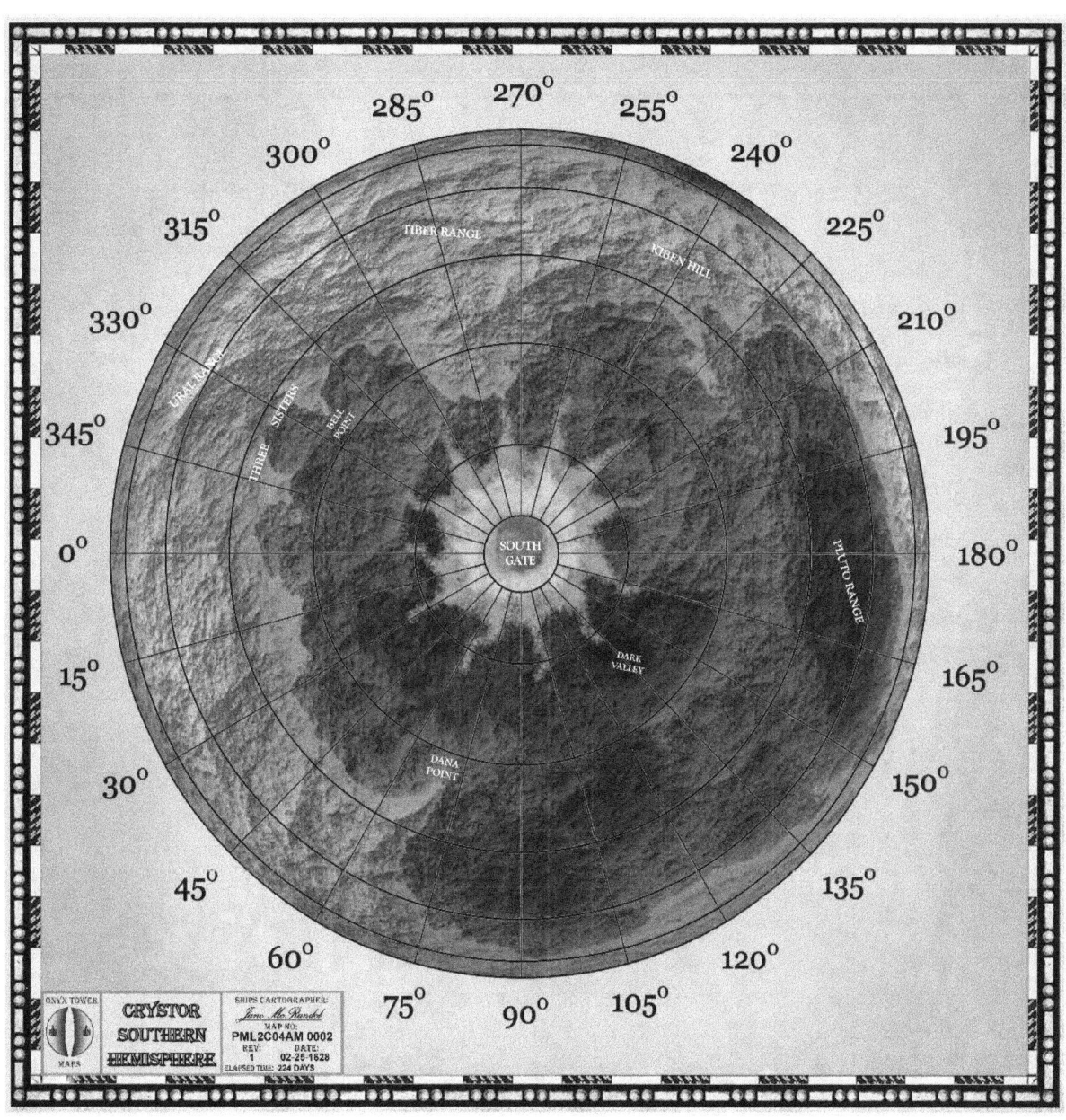

68. CRYSTOR SOUTHERN HEMISPHERE that always faces Pangaea.

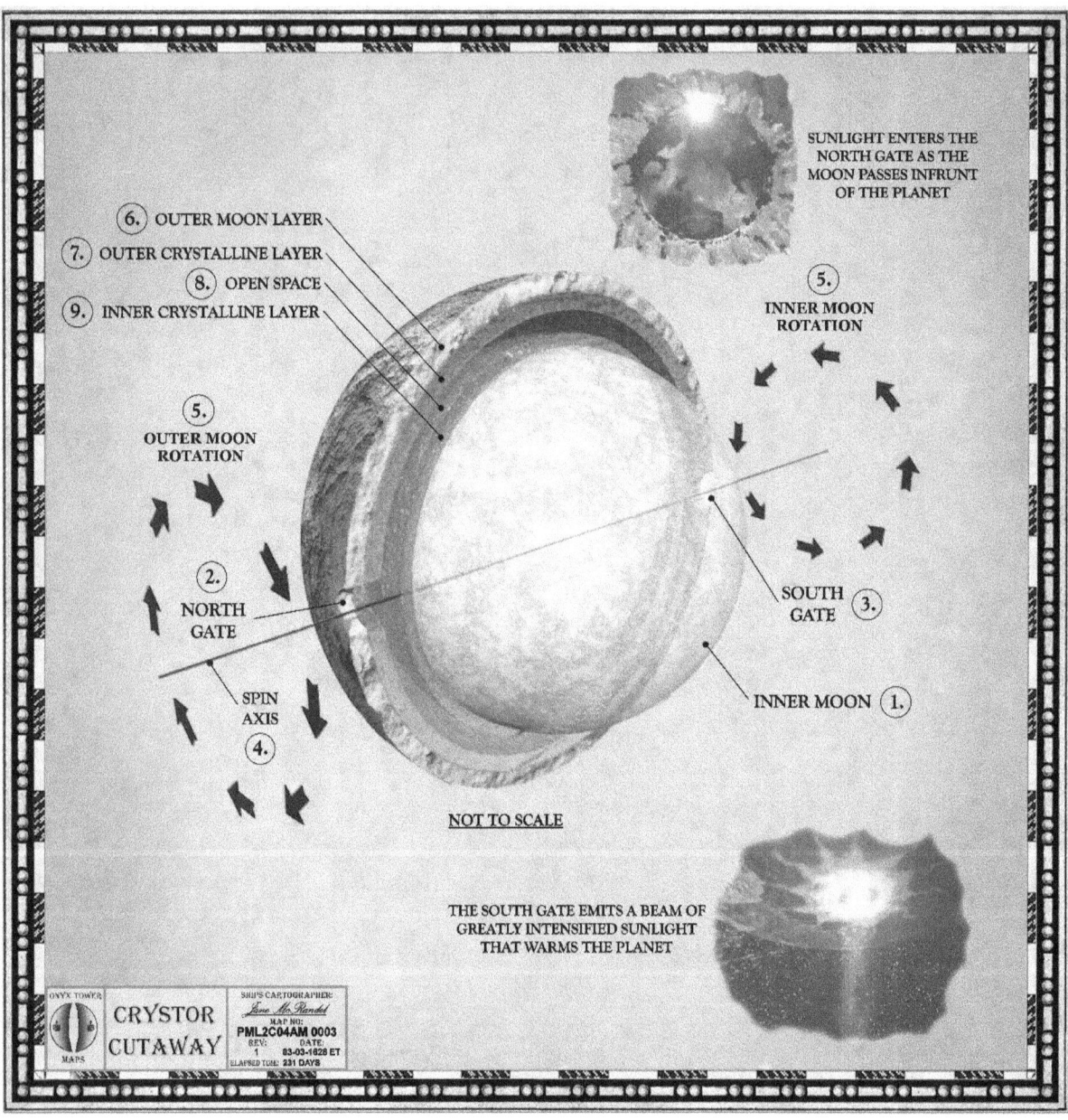

SUNLIGHT ENTERS THE
NORTH GATE AS THE
MOON PASSES INFRUNT
OF THE PLANET

6. OUTER MOON LAYER
7. OUTER CRYSTALLINE LAYER
8. OPEN SPACE
9. INNER CRYSTALLINE LAYER

5. INNER MOON ROTATION

5. OUTER MOON ROTATION

2. NORTH GATE

SOUTH GATE 3.

SPIN AXIS
4.

INNER MOON 1.

NOT TO SCALE

THE SOUTH GATE EMITS A BEAM OF
GREATLY INTENSIFIED SUNLIGHT
THAT WARMS THE PLANET

ONYX TOWER
MAPS

CRYSTOR
CUTAWAY

SHIP'S CARTOGRAPHER:
Lane Mc Randel
MAP NO:
PML2C04AM 0003
REV: 1   DATE: 03-03-1828 ET
ELAPSED TIME: 231 DAYS

69. LIONHEART WANTED THE INTERIOR of Crystor documented as best as it could be based on their passage through it. McRandel created a cutaway drawing that was not to scale. **1. Inner Moon:** is believed to be hollow due to the moon's low mass. It is also thought to have an automated internal drive in place that keeps the spin axis pointed directly at the center of the planet it orbits. **2. North Gate:** is the opening on the moon's north pole that collects sunlight as the moon's far side passes between the planet and the sun. **3. South Gate:** is the opening on the moon's south pole the emits an intense, magnified beam of the sun's energy onto the planet as the moon passes in front of the sun. Without the periodic beam, the average temperature of the planet would fall below freezing. **4. Spin Axis:** constantly adjusts to remain pointed directly toward the planet's center at all times as the moon orbits. **5. Outer and Inner Moon Rotation:** The opposite rotation of the outer and inner moons acts as a generator to dramatically increase the energy of the sun's rays as the moon passes between the planet and the sun. **6. Outer Moon Layer:** The outer moon diameter measures 2,237 miles [3600 km]. **7. Outer Crystalline Layer:** Engineer Petrov referred to this layer as the "Stator Layer". The inner surface of the outer crystalline layer diameter measures approximately 2,197 miles [3,535.7 km]. **8. Open Space:** The space gap between the outer and inner crystalline layers measures approximately 10 miles [16.1 km]. **9. Inner Crystalline Layer:** Engineer Petrov referred to this layer as the "Armature Layer". It is thought to be approximately 10 miles [16.1 km] thick. The diameter of the inner moon below the inner crystal layer is believed to be approximately 2,157 miles [3471.4 km].

Captains Log: Our voyage elapsed time is now 168days (Dec 9th, 1627, Earth Time)

12:00 Hours:

We managed to make repairs to the ship, and it is now fully operational. For the first time, our ability to fabricate material from natural resources and the material remains from the nearby ruins of the underground city has been put to the test. A modest transparent recreation dome is now in place where dome three was blown up. We won't know if it is fully secure until the tower returns to space, but it's my guess well find that out soon enough.

I'm haunted by news received from West. After extensive work on the signal that beckoned us inside the energy moon, she has determined that it was a warning. One that was coming from my voice. It would seem at some point; my future self is going to be exposed to or able to broadcast to a previous time. I guess I shouldn't be surprised, since this voyage began, time hasn't been linear.

The dreams of voices calling out to me from the darkness continue. Even though we've only discovered ancient, absolute destruction, I can't escape the feeling that we are not alone. There's something here. We will be moving on to explore other areas of interest very soon.

P. M. Lionheart: Captain

70. LIONHEART AND WEST look out from the newly completed structure that replaced dome three.

The End

The **Illustrated Tales From An Alternate Steampunk History** series is based on a collection of stories that were posted online over a period of several years. These stories cover the lives of characters, both good and evil, human, and non-human, natural or created, and some that live between the centuries. Throughout the timeline their lives and actions set off a chain reaction of events that create an extraordinary woven pattern of history that spans from the time of ancient periods to the centuries that lay ahead. The series is not limited to Earth or Human history, but also covers non-human, off-world events, some of which had an influence on humanity. Because of my interest in Steampunk, several stories take place in the 19th century where: genetic engineering, terraforming, and faster than light drive have become a reality with unexpected treasures and consequences.

ALSO AVAILABLE:

Tim Dooley's interest in 19th century science fiction goes back to the late 1950's after seeing the movie "The Fabulous World of Jules Verne". During the 70's and 80's, he illustrated fantasy machines that included airships, land steamers, flying machines, submarine steamships, off-world cities, planetary and interstellar spacecraft. In 1986 these drawings created an opportunity for him to work as a designer in the aerospace industry. In 1994, his drawings caught the attention of the woman who later became his wife. In 1997, one of his airship drawings was published in the Orange County Register's Focus on Science page. In 2003, he started creating scratch-built models of his own designs for what he called "The Jules Verne Room". Over the years he posted illustrated stories all of which were based on an alternate steampunk timeline and is now in the process of converting those stories into semi-graphic books.

www.ingramcontent.com/pod-product-compliance
Lightning Source LLC
Chambersburg PA
CBHW081247210626
46818CB00016B/3105